Joan Marysmith lives in Leicester with her husband; her three children are now grown up and live in London. She is the financial director of the family business, but hopes to retire quite soon, and spend more time writing. She has written more than a dozen children's books but it was only after she completed an Open University degree that she felt able to attempt her first novel, *Holy Aspic*. She is fond of travel, especially by train, having crossed Siberia on the Trans-Siberian railway, and more recently gone from Samarkand to Shanghai across central China.

D1114416

# HOLY ASPIC

## Joan Marysmith

**BLACK SWAN**

**HOLY ASPIC**
**A BLACK SWAN BOOK : 0 552 99688 2**

First publication in Great Britain

PRINTING HISTORY
Black Swan edition published 1996

Copyright © Joan Marysmith 1996

The right of Joan Marysmith to be identified as the author of this
work has been asserted in accordance with sections 77 and 78
of the Copyright Designs and Patents Act 1988.

All of the characters in this book are fictitious,
and any resemblance to actual persons, living or dead,
is purely coincidental.

*Condition of Sale*
This book is sold subject to the condition that it shall not, by way of
trade or otherwise, be lent, re-sold, hired out or otherwise circulated in
any form of binding or cover other than that in which it is published
and without a similar condition including this condition being
imposed on the subsequent purchaser.

Set in 11/13pt Linotype Melior by
Phoenix typesetting, Ilkley, West Yorkshire

Black Swan Books are published by Transworld Publishers Ltd,
61-63 Uxbridge Road, London W5 5SA,
in Australia by Transworld Publishers (Australia) Pty Ltd,
15-25 Helles Avenue, Moorebank, NSW 2170
and in New Zealand by Transworld Publishers (NZ) Ltd,
3 William Pickering Drive, Albany, Auckland.

Reproduced, printed and bound in Great Britain by
Cox & Wyman Ltd, Reading, Berks.

For David,
who is nothing like Hughie

# Chapter One

Fenn Meadowcroft walked into Corrigan's fresh fish bar, only to avoid the Vicar.

From there, through the fronds of plastic seaweed, fanned gracefully across the window, she watched William come into view. His defensive, denim-blue eyes were fixed on the pavement. His hair, so pale, fell forward straight from the parting, making him look younger than he was. It contrasted starkly with his black clerical cloak, billowing and swelling in the wind.

Unfortunately, he felt her gaze, and looked in through the window. Fenn hastily inspected the fish spread out before her, flaccid and slippery, on the refrigerated slabs. She examined the uncouth face of the John Dory, the alarming flicker of movement from a boiled crab, and a small notice, which said 'Fish makes brains'. She leaned over the slab, holding her coat to her, head tilted back, trying not to breathe in the smell of salt and scales.

'Received wisdom,' she said, pointing to the notice. 'No-one's proved that fish has any influence on intelligence.'

'It encourages the mothers,' said Corrigan. He let her browse. He liked Mrs Meadowcroft. She never wore lipstick, and her face was very pale, like a cameo, though the nose wasn't at all classical, more perky, the way it turned up. He even liked her untidy hair, the colour of a healthy red setter puppy, slightly elegant, and about as wayward. Today, it was tugged together in an ineffectual knot at the back of her head. Gently, and absent-mindedly, he stroked a halibut.

Fenn glanced towards the window, careful not to focus fully on it. She could see William, stooping against the January wind, hovering, waiting for her to emerge. She would have to buy.

'Plaice or haddock?' asked Corrigan. He had a sheet of film at the ready.

'No,' she said. 'No. Not plaice. Not haddock. I'll have skate wings today. Those two large ones, please.'

'Something different, is it?'

'I think so.' She glanced again at the window. 'Gawd,' she said, 'he's still lurking.'

Fenn came out of Corrigan's, wedging the parcel into her basket. 'Hello William.' She tried to sound surprised.

'Long time, no see.' The informality was at odds with his mysterious, swirling mantle, and especially with the antique silver double clasp, holding it together.

'I haven't been to church much lately, if that's what you mean,' said Fenn. She meant to be gentle, but the expression of concern which William had pasted on his face since spotting her, was not endearing.

'I miss you warbling away merrily. It must be a couple of months now.'

'We came at Christmas.'

'Don't you all?'

'Don't worry. It's not your sermons.' She pushed back a frond of hair from her eyes.

'Do we have a problem?' His pale blue eyes looked optimistic.

'No. Absolutely not.'

'I wish you'd do the flowers again. The chancel

pedestal wobbled perilously during the *Te Deum* last Sunday. Of course, the boy sopranos are exceptionally strong at the moment.' William raised one eyebrow, a mannerism often charming, but in William's case, making him look like a twitchy hamster, busy and fastidious.

Fenn shook her head, and the knot of her hair nearly unsprung itself.

'What about popping in tomorrow? Epiphany. I've got a very good joke I'm slipping into the sermon. Expect it will pass unnoticed, as usual. Bring Hughie. Stiffen him up spiritually, for the new term.'

William always liked to see Hughie in church. He made up for spasmodic attendance by enthusiasm, singing the hymns with total disregard to the pace of the choir. Hughie made the place feel fuller than it really was.

'I'll do my best.' Fenn tried to sound unhopeful.

'God bless.'

'I wouldn't put money on it.'

'What . . . ?' William watched her stride away, the knot of hair bouncing from side to side, losing more strands. He frowned, the look of concern slipping. He'd always considered Fenn Meadowcroft to be such an orderly woman.

William made too many assumptions, Fenn thought, he was too certain about received wisdom. Presumably, he'd be quite happy with 'fish makes brains'. There are some things you believe for years, until you find out they're not true, and never were.

Fenn discovered uncertainty when her cousin's son, Ray, had the accident. It was his birthday today, that's why he was on her mind. For two years now, he'd lain in a hospital bed in Adelaide. The driver who hit him got six months. Ray had been captain of Rugby at fifteen, he, an English boy in an Australian school. Now, he could move only his left arm. Ray, who'd played the computer keys like a young Mozart, master of the Random Access Memory, now drifted unknowingly in the fringeland of the mind, fleetingly surfacing to the world, but, for the most part, elsewhere. He was twenty-one years old, and should have been dancing the night away at this very moment, celebrating his maturity. Instead, he may have opened his eyes, reached out with his clawed left hand, even struggled for a word; giving out more signs that he was far too alive to have the machine switched off. None of which man would have allowed, if man had been a loving and compassionate god.

Since Fenn had become uncertain of a loving God, because of Ray, other instances of such negligence seemed everywhere, in newspapers, on the telly, in the experiences of friends. Yet, she couldn't believe in a god who was not good. It would put civilization back two thousand years.

Fenn lived at the far end of Springfield Lane, on the curve. It was an attractive road, but not fashionable, being on the wrong side of the town. The decent sized Victorian houses had character, which was a polite way of saying they were on the shabby side. They lacked the elegance of the south, there were no Georgian proportions here, but neither were there the cold grey stones of the North. Fenn had always been happy with the Midlands.

She could see already the sash windows looking out over the holly hedge, and knew that beside the peacock-blue front door, the pale lemon witch hazel was in flower, mysterious in its form, and so fragrant that she could smell it a yard away.

It began to rain, icy drizzles stabbing spitefully at her forehead. She turned up her coat collar, and shook her head. The insecure knot of hair released itself in a single bound, and blew, momentarily, high above her head, then subsided across her face. She laughed with surprise, and shook it back from her eyes. Then, like the Vicar, she put her head down to angle her face from the cold.

Fenn set aside the thought of Ray and considered if she should cook the skate wings with black butter and capers, or braise them in the oven which might suit Hughie better.

She was level with one of the larger houses, with narrow pointed gables, which had been converted into flats. As she was looking at the ground, Fenn didn't notice the man coming the other way.

They collided head on.

Fenn sprang back. 'Ooops. Sorry, my fault,' she said.

The man was no taller than herself, neither young nor old, but his oversized black coat gave him import. It emphasized his dark hair and unshaven chin. He had that carelessness about him, seen in successful men who need make no effort to impress. Men, that is, who are successful with women, dangerous sports, or pop music, but who are rarely accountants or dentists. His heavy eyelids were scornful, impatient, superior, as he stared at her, automatically insolent. Then he almost smiled, a lazy realignment of a long nose and heavy top lip.

'Mmm,' he said.

That was it. With no apology, he moved to the left, and walked up the drive of the house behind her, the lazy sway of his shoulders reinforcing her first impression of moody arrogance.

Fenn couldn't help smiling, too. The totally un-expected, small murmur was merely a witty little compliment, nothing crude or physical. The smile

11

was not a leer, not a threat. It said many things, yet meant nothing. A joke. A drop of precious oil, which smoothed her day. He was certainly not a man who could be confused with the Vicar.

The rain felt fresh and cool on her face, no longer biting.

## Chapter Two

'Hughie,' called Fenn, 'Tea. Tea everyone.' The tray was on the small gateleg by the window, tea poured. Several slabs of Christmas cake were propped up against each other, like paving stones waiting to be laid.

The house lent itself well to Christmas. There was a *gravitas* about the mahogany stair rail that looked solid under swags of yew. The ceilings were high enough for a decent-sized tree, the window ledges wide for creations of ivy and hellebores. Though now, of course, the pine needles clattered about when she hoovered, and the hellebores clearly regretted being indoors.

Sometimes, Fenn felt the house had created her, lent order and meaning to her life. Sometimes, she wondered if Hughie had been her escape. Other people had thought Mummy wonderful, so eccentric, so attractive to men. Fenn knew how it felt to have Uncles, who were there only for a year or two, to spend months in foreign houses, to lie awake while the parties got noisier. She and Pru had been Mummy's accessories, proof of her nurturing qualities, yet never her rivals.

Fenn drank her tea, grateful for its warmth. Her hair was now tidily into a bun at the nape of her neck. Lunch had been tedious, all that fuss about the skate wings, each cut into half. Too innovative for Hughie. Too many bones for Pru. Not enough flesh for Damaris. They left the capers, and Damaris had a row with Pru about the Virgin birth. Fenn often wondered how she, so reasonable and undemanding, came to have a daughter like Damaris, and a sister like Pru.

Damaris had been difficult from the first confrontations over potty training, but as a small child she'd soothed away her own anguish with an ever ready and charming smile. This attractive feature was now kept for use strictly outside the home. Pru, on the other hand, had only recently become difficult. She was younger than Fenn by five years, but they'd got on well as children, Pru being old for her age. She seemed to enjoy her work with a legal firm in Ealing, proud of her career-girl status, at ease with her freedom. But now, when she came to stay, she'd grown critical, too eager to borrow a duster to clean up, not enthusiastic enough about the food. Pru needed domesticity. Pru needed a man.

To calm herself, Fenn spent the afternoon updating her recipe file on the computer in the kitchen, and put together three spring menus for her business lunches. She deleted the one with a prawn cocktail starter. Damaris was nowhere to be seen. Pru had volunteered to do the ironing, saying she never got to do shirts and pyjamas. Slowly, the sense of order, of being in control, had prevailed, and by the time tea was ready, Fenn was able to look out of the sitting-room window, over the darkening garden, with a sense of peace.

'Mum?' bellowed Damaris from the landing.

'I'm downstairs, darling,' said Fenn in a deliberately calm tone, ever hopeful that moderation would rub off.

'I'll kill whoever's done this,' said Damaris, erupting into the room like a blast from Vesuvius. She threw a pair of jeans onto the sofa. She was swathed in black

14

cheesecloth, in contrast to her face which was chalk-white. The only colour was in her hair, which reflected a curious tangerine glow under the light.

'I had to wash them,' Fenn said, ready to be reasonable. 'It comes to that, now and again.' Damaris had to be handled with care, she blew so easily. Her hair, thought Fenn, looked like the back end of a wet hen. A foreign wet hen.

'There's no holes,' wailed Damaris. 'I don't mind them being clean. But you've mended both knees. They haven't LIVED.'

'I think your Aunt Pru must have been at the knees.'

'She only came yesterday. I've had enough already. She's ruining my life. She's a middle-class pleb.'

'Try not to contradict yourself. Pru likes to serve others. That's her gift, I'm afraid. Where is she now?'

'Gone to get what she calls a proper loaf. To make pilchard sandwiches. She doesn't like medium sliced. And she didn't rate the stingray for lunch. Me neither.'

'So you said.'

Damaris picked up the cake knife, and started to hack at the patches. 'At least when I get to Australia there won't be Pru to plague me. When me and Marie get to the beach barbies, you won't recognize us. We'll be out of this dump. Living, at last.'

'You're not there yet. Many more threats like that, and you won't be. Besides, you may have passed your retakes.'

'Forget it. There's more chance of a cat mating on a telephone wire.'

The jagged rents restored to the jeans, Damaris retreated to the hall, sat on the floor hunched up against the radiator, the phone in her lap, dialling out, to find out what was on for the evening.

Fenn breathed deeply, and tried to feel in touch with the fleeting peace. She failed. Damaris was bad enough normally, but Pru did make everything worse. Fenn decided Pru's moods were down to sexual frustration.

If only she could reach out and warm Pru, heal the pain. Pru's path was strewn with chunks of agony, great boulders of gloom. It wasn't for want of prayer, good quality prayer, unselfish, generous, trusting and sincere prayer. All Pru wanted was quite an ordinary man. We're not asking for Melvyn Bragg, merely some quiet little soul, who's looking for a good home, Fenn had explained to the Almighty on more than one occasion. You could say that Pru was yet another nail in God's coffin.

Fenn sighed, and started to de-bauble the tree.

Hughie escaped to the study after lunch, and lay sideways on the sofa, a cushion covering his uppermost ear. His hair, which needed cutting, tickled his neck. The cushion enveloped him in a dusty smell, an integral part of the room. Fenn wasn't encouraged to waft her dusters, or spread her beeswax here, there was too much to disturb. He moved the cat, sometimes called Vodka, other times Mysterium, from where she lay curled up in the corner of the sofa. She stamped about on the spot for a bit, then climbed on top of him, coiling herself into a warm and comforting presence. He stroked her, aware of her bones through the fur, and her watchful, green and insolent eyes.

Lunch, with Damaris, Pru and skate together, had been almost too much. He'd never encountered skate before, and its form was profoundly disturbing, worryingly un-fishlike. He breathed deeply five times, ignoring the dust, and reached out for the comfort of a book. There were those on the table that had been presents at Christmas. He picked up the George Eliot biography. A remarkable woman, George Eliot, though daunting beyond belief.

He sighed, and knew himself to be a lucky man. This room was the womb from which he'd come, the nest to which he would always return, his sanctuary. He speculated whether he was mixing his metaphors, or if he were marrying up womb and nest in rather a clever way. He'd always known this room, it was part of the family house. His father had been the Reverend here, and then bought the property when a new and cheaper vicarage had been built.

Hughie was also lucky to be Head of English at St Anthony's, where the boys had enough native wit to misspend their days quietly, rather than distract authoritarian teaching with sheath knives, or catapults made out of desk brackets and condoms. Hughie was aware of such incidents, because they featured in the newspapers favoured by the younger staff on the science side.

He heard Fenn call, even through the cushion. He marked the page he was at with a piece of ribbon that had once tied up Damaris's hair as a child. Eventually, after rearranging his Christmas books in the order in which he intended to read them, he got himself to the sitting-room.

Hughie smiled at Fenn indulgently, thinking how capable she looked, standing on a dining-room chair, getting the fairy off the top of the tree. Her hands were rather large, definitely competent, and still freckled, as they were in the summer. He knew their touch, how they could soothe. They could iron all the pain out of his neck, when he got stressed over the exam results.

Her hair gleamed under the light. It was the hair he'd first noticed, and still he liked her to keep it long. Now she was older, its length was disguised in a variety of knots and loops. Only he knew how it looked spread over the pillow. She was proof of his own reliability; a sensible and attractive woman like that wouldn't have married a fool. She did, however, look tense.

'Damaris,' Fenn said, stretching up to reach the top of the tree, 'is the pits.' She threw the fairy down for him to catch. He took it well, like a cricket ball, pulling it into his chest with both hands.

'What will she get up to in Australia?' Fenn said, tugging angrily at the small Santa laden with a golf bag. 'She's off the leash already, and Australia's the land of opportunity.'

Hughie was pleased with his catch, and threw the fairy up in the air once more, to relish the co-ordination of eye and hand.

'Look out, Hughie. You've squashed its wing.' Fenn looked down from the height of the chair, and momentarily closed her eyes in despair. Why did she always have to be in charge? Why didn't Hughie worry about Damaris, as she did? Why did he have to play silly games with the decorations?

Inexplicably, the face of the man she'd bumped into that morning came into her mind. Moody and difficult, he looked. But fun. And he'd be in charge. Alive. She smiled again at his small, affirmative grunt. A little semi-grin, a tiny joke, insignificant incidents which reach out, and momentarily warm.

'A splendid catch. I was firm and resolute. Never a butterfingers.' Gently, he smoothed out the wing, careful not to inflict further damage. They'd had that fairy a long time. A different, more modern fairy, wouldn't be right.

Fenn, having cleared the top of the tree, climbed down and began to wrap the crib figures up in tissue. 'It's always the same, Christmas, isn't it? A long way from Bethlehem.'

'It wasn't exactly the same. I behaved very well over the coriander stuffing. I tried hard to get it down.'

18

The door opened slowly and a tray came into view. 'Tea time,' called Pru from behind it. She came cautiously into the room, sliding her feet enquiringly over the carpet, as if she were walking in the dark. The tray was laden with sandwiches, teapot, cups, and jam tarts in three colours, from out of a cardboard box. 'Pilchard *and* cucumber,' said Pru, pointing with her chin to the sandwiches. There was a smear of Flora on her otherwise unadorned chin.

'Another tea,' said Fenn, glancing at the tray she'd brought in earlier. 'A pity it's Dodo's party tonight.'

Pru staggered with her burden to the sofa table. 'Oh dear, you've done it already. It must have been while I was shopping.' Her hopeful smile turned to disappointment. She had so wanted to help. 'Sorry.'

'It looks lovely,' said Hughie, whose propping up of his sister-in-law was fairly automatic. 'It's just a shame Dodo's party will come on top of it.'

'A party's a party,' said Pru. 'A chance to get out. By the way, since it's been tipping down all day, I thought you might need your umbrella, so I've washed it.' Pru had obviously found a few empty minutes during the afternoon, and filled them with service to another.

'It gets washed when it rains,' said Hughie.

'Not with ecologically-sound detergent.' She handed it to him, proud of the neat furls which might have been ironed. The wooden handle now bore a sickly white bloom. She leaned hopefully towards him, anxious for approval. Her hand-cut fringe, childlike and severe, demanded some response.

'Thank you, Pru.' Hughie was energetically grateful. Pru always made him feel guilty. The faded black fabric had lost its rust stains and familiar patina. The handle was as dead bone. His umbrella had become a stranger. He took it to the porch and found Damaris going out through the front door.

19

'I'm going to have tea with May,' she said. 'At least May listens when I speak.'

'We've got two teas here. There are thousands of sandwiches.'

'Your prob, Popkin. If there's anything gritty in them, it'll be cyanide.'

'Cyanide is a liquid.'

'I wouldn't put anything past that woman. You want to watch her. You should see what she did to my jeans. She'll be sewing up your zip next.'

Hughie returned to the sitting-room and briefly brushed Fenn's arm as he walked past. Thank heavens Fenn was as she was, capable, and always the same. Without Fenn to lend order to his life, he would be as flotsam cast upon the shore.

As she knew she must, Fenn leaned forward to catch his eye, to tell him silently that his world was safe. As the surrendering of milk to a baby brings consolation to the mother, so reassuring Hughie soothed Fenn, brought its own comfort.

'Haven't had pilchards in years,' she said to Pru, and energetically ate two of the sandwiches. It was the least she could do.

Only then, and for no reason, did she give any consideration to the party. Dodo's flat was in the Victorian house into which the man in the enveloping overcoat had gone that morning.

# Chapter Three

May Lomax sat upright in her winged arm chair, with her feet together, and the tea tray on a low, rattan table in front of her. The room was cosy, with restrained light from two lamps. The advantage of a flat in an old house was that you got decent-sized rooms without there being too many of them.

Hers was the ground-floor flat, so the kitchen was where it was meant to be. The dining-room had become her bedroom. It was at the back, and she'd had the french doors made into an English window for safety reasons. It had, after fifteen years, become a real home. Its dust was her dust, the molecules of air had all probably been part of her being, she was at one with her environment.

May was especially happy. Damaris had chosen to visit. To visit HER, May, a bud near withered on the stem, without ever having come to fruit, one of life's least significant passengers. Moreover, May managed to produce a proper tea, with Earl Grey, scones, and Damaris's little savoury favourite, all coming together at the proper time, at dusk, on a winter afternoon. It was an achievement, so much could go wrong. Things conspired. One small lapse, and it could have been cocoa in the teapot, or furniture cream on the scones. Just to be certain, May lifted the teapot lid, and was reassured.

When Damaris wasn't looking, she flicked the middle finger of her left hand across the surface of one scone, and tested the flavour on her tongue. All was well.

'Is it all right, dear?' May watched anxiously as Damaris forced her fork into the Royal Worcester ramekin dish. She wondered why she used to imagine that Damaris was how little Rose would have been, had she lived. Damaris had been such a pretty child, of course. For years, May had deliberately confused Damaris with Rose in her memory, it had helped to keep the picture of her departed child vibrant.

These days, more often, the images of Rose and Damaris diverged, with May praying that Damaris would soon turn the corner. With Christmas only just gone, with new hope coming into the world to sustain them all, Damaris did appear, today, to be reasonably congenial, though strangely attired. Her T-shirt was gorilla sized, the jeans quite worn away around the knee.

Damaris took a forkful of the salmon mousse, and chewed it, for longer than seemed necessary, with her eyes closed.

'Fine,' she eventually said.

'I thought it might be a little too sturdy?'

'It's fine.'

'Gelatine isn't easy to judge.'

'I thought you'd done a different sort of mousse when I came in. The hall stinks of kippers.'

'I'm afraid it's not quite gone, the smell. It was silly of me. Somehow, they got into the toaster. So easily done, of course.'

'You'll have to concentrate more,' said Damaris, 'or the Social Services will get you.'

May shivered. Mishaps, she knew, would lead to care and interference. She could never leave her garden, and the rattan chairs that had once graced the veranda of her parents' bungalow in Simla, that lovely low house which clung to the hillside like a mollusc, and was so high you could see the whole curve of the town in the hills. Leave them, and live in one of those places, ridiculously called Homes?

'The Social Services won't get in my way,' said May, briskly shaking scone crumbs from her lace jabot, brushing them under the sofa with her foot. 'They haven't had the upbringing.' She smiled, musing on the lack of well-modulated vowels among many in the so-called caring services. 'The Community Nurse, to give but one example, sounds to be from the least well-drained part of Lincolnshire.'

'Mee-ow.'

'I know. I shouldn't. But I always have. Been on the tart side. There are things I regret, of course. And it's not very Christian. But deeply satisfying.'

'Mum says you'll be all right so long as you keep your act together.' Damaris wiped her nose with the back of her hand, and dried it against her jeans. 'Why did you ask me to come to tea today? Is it special?'

'Rose would be fifty today. Not a little girl any more. Children of her own. My grandchildren. Pretty little things with curls and warm hands to hold. Or would they be great-grandchildren I'm thinking of?'

''Spec' so,' said Damaris, and still annoyed with Pru, leaned forward, and tugged at the gash in her jeans at the left knee.

May sighed. Life nowadays was empty of warmth and of laughter. Its problems spread themselves to take up more of the day, small and unimportant though they might be, like not being able to get her feet in the wash basin now, in the mornings.

'Are you going to Dodo's tonight?' Damaris knew she had to make some sort of effort for the poor old thing. 'Popkin's pretty pissed off with the idea.'

'Of course I'm going. A party at my age. What fun. And only to the flat upstairs. No taxi expense.'

'I think Dodo's after the new inmate myself. The one just moved into the top. Randy cow, that's what she is. I saw him yesterday. Thinks he's God's gift to women. Got a very knowing walk. Know what I mean?'

'Don't talk like that, Rose. Dodo is not remotely bovine. I imagine divorcees have their needs. They don't have the same loyalty as a widow.'

'You can tell. She's taken to wearing larger earrings, and there was yoghurt with the milk on the step yesterday, to make her look healthy.'

'I always preferred tennis parties myself,' May said. 'Was really rather good with a racquet. Never a cross word in those days. Very good sports, everyone was. Did I tell you about meeting Tom?'

'I've got to be going,' said Damaris quickly, sensing the past coming on. Seeing May's flicker of regret, she added, 'No-one does a salmon mousse like you do. Thanks.'

'It's wrong to live in the past, isn't it?' May tried to keep her tone light, not to let the question sound like a plea for reassurance.

'No. You're OK in the past. It's the present you've got to be careful with. Tell you what,' said Damaris. 'Promise you'll do me salmon mousse when I get back from Australia. Yes?'

'Of course I will, dear. We'll have our own special celebration. If I'm still here.' May laughed with anticipation, and Damaris was surprised, once again, how strangely her face changed when it was no longer anxious. Her nostrils shot up a full centimetre, squashing her smooth little cheeks into two pink snooker balls. Weird, thought Damaris, because she might have been quite pretty when she was young.

Gliding purposefully to the door, like a three-dimensional shadow, Damaris let herself out, without allowing the possibility of further reminiscence. The door slammed with an uncaring thud. May looked at the ramekin of salmon mousse, only half eaten, and already beginning to tarnish at the edge.

Determined not to feel empty, May turned off the lamp and sat looking out at the dark street. She'd met dear Tom at a tennis party. Dearest Tom. Fifteen years now, alone. She'd liked tennis parties better than dances, though she'd been good on her feet. There was always the worry about being asked, especially for her favourites like the Military Two Step, and the Gay Gordons. Well, there's a dance that won't come back. Not among decent people, anyway.

The family had liked Tom, he was such a gentleman, even though marrying him meant living in a smaller house than she'd been used to. I never minded that at all. And I'm lucky to have this flat now, because of the garden. A real garden. All the nicer because Dodo never wants anything to do with it. The new man in the top flat doesn't look the gardening type either, thank goodness. Rather an unusual fellow, to say the least. Bohemian, perhaps. No-one could say that poor old May didn't see life in its infinite variety, now that she was reduced to flat residency.

May slightly relaxed her posture, allowing her head to rest against the high back of the chair. Mustn't stay too late she told herself. Church to look forward to tomorrow, Epiphany. What a wicked man, the Bishop of Durham, trying to make out there never had been any Wise Men. Ridiculous. They'd been one of the clearest signals of the Saviour's divinity.

She remembered she must mend her evening bag. The fastener was loose. She'd always had that bag, since she was married, even before she was married. It had come into and gone out of fashion, like the tide. She no longer cared whether it was an in, or out time for beaded *pochettes*. She'd even had that bag when she'd known Lewis.

Lewis, who was long before she met Tom. She might have married Lewis. How different her life would have been if she had. Didn't know the meaning of the word sensible. She'd made a terrible mess of things when he'd asked her. It might have been fate, but it wasn't. It was May herself, not forgetful in those days, but stubborn.

She always spent time sitting around like this, waiting for him, he was so unreliable and always late. And so left wing. She would never have met Lewis at a tennis party. No, it was on a train. Not that he picked her up, of course, but after he'd been talking to her, he sat writing a letter. She could still see his hand, tanned from walking in Spain, as he wrote, and the way his mouth, wide and quirky, moved slightly as he worked out what to write.

She was amazed when he handed her the letter as she got off the train. He asked her to write to him, because, he said, he liked the way her nose wobbled when she laughed.

He hadn't approved of us being in India at all, but then the family hadn't approved of Lewis either. No background, they said. May tried to say everyone had a background, but they insisted that wasn't the same thing. There was never a quarrel. But there were always the differences that got in the way of understanding. Because he was so aggressive, May needed to be firm, to keep her end up as it were. When you're young it's impossible to see the way round differences, even when other things were so right. He used to buy her, though not often, three yellow carnations. Always three, for the varying ways he loved her, he said. But the differences had won in the end, because both Lewis and May had been too young to see clearly.

So she married dear Tom. How happy they were, doing everything together, no misunderstandings all their lives. He wished they could be back in India too, so they helped each other be strong about that. A perfect life, except for the tragedy of Rose. A terrible disease, but she hadn't suffered. Even then, they made a useful life together without children.

May stood up unsteadily, and paused for a moment to allow her spent bones to recognize what action was required of them. She turned on the lamp and went to draw the curtains, leaving Tom, Rose, and Lewis in her other world. Tom and Rose faded as quickly as summer.

So why was it she could still see Lewis so clearly?

Two floors above her, in the top flat, Lex Fielding concentrated on the VDU, as if expecting the text to appear, extracted by undiscovered forces, from the turbulent and swirling morass of his mind. Actually he was putting off the moment when he must go to the flat below, and face Dodo's party, to say nothing of Dodo herself. Lex knew himself to be a complex and interesting man. He made certain of it. He cultivated seeming to be laid back. He also knew a predatory woman when he saw one.

He sighed. The chapter waited to be written. It existed. It was truth. It needed merely to be plucked from the air. As a statue existed potentially within the marble, before it was revealed by the chisel, so the chapter lived, waiting to be defined by the word. This book was his gospel. On its emergence into print, like a butterfly struggling from its chrysalis, Lex would be transmogrified. He would be seen in his true light, an intellectual, a guru, a pivotal force. He would give up teaching, and write about teaching instead. He would be an arty person.

Structured debate was the key to this damned book. The world would change beyond recognition if the ordinary man could be made to think for himself.

Tentatively, pecking at the keys with the middle fingers of each hand, he produced, 'Christianity is the scourge of philosophy. Hot lines from God are not a proven source of ethical certainty.'

He put his fingertips on either side of his forehead, fingering his slightly receding hairline, and closed his eyes. The writing was awful. Far too chatty. He must get it right. Civilization could move no further forward if it were tied to fanciful and irrational fictions.

He sat back and looked around him for inspiration. He liked the simplicity of this flat, high above the trees, with its motley furniture, and a minimum of it. Dodo, who owned the whole house, and so was his landlady, left no trace here of her plenitude, of the dedication to lush comfort that she herself exuded. The imitation teak table, the moulded plastic chair had long since ceased to exist in even the cheapest store. Lex liked the anonymity, the Spartan sparsity of furniture; it seemed necessary for his creative flowering. He hoped he would not be here for long.

Suddenly, going to Dodo's party seemed easier than wrestling with his book. Lex saved the file, and logged out. He made a mug of tea, boiling water in the egg pan, and was pleasantly surprised to find a nutty bar abandoned earlier on the telephone table. He took the decision that a shave could only improve him. There is designer stubble, and there is the slovenly look. Youth, and star status are required to produce the former.

In the bathroom mirror, he saw a man driven by fate; Byronic, he decided, ridden restlessly by the muse.

Against the odds too, for he was not a philosopher. English was his burden. Some might think him a fool. He knew beyond possible doubt that he was a catalyst for change, a force who would not pass unremarked. He woke every morning, wondering if this were the day when he would effect a transformation.

For a man with the Socratic turn of mind, it was strange that he didn't ask why he believed this. That it might have been the result of his mother's lack of care, a lack of pride in him, the absence of the gift of self worth, which had led him to follow, so aggressively, the need for recognition. He never enquired.

Perhaps that was not so. After all, Granpy had proved a good mother as well as grandfather. He'd fed him on egg and chips, when he'd gone round, living only next door, read him Hardy and Virginia Woolf, and taught him to love them both, and made certain he got to university, albeit Leicester, not Cambridge.

Lex was a man driven, but for all that, not an unhappy one. After only one week in the area, he was being lured into the middle flat by this Dodo woman, fleshly and husky-voiced she was, though no chicken. He was to be looked over. He was to be assessed, mentally undressed. Was possibly to be seduced; he knew a hungry woman when he saw one. He took a shower, just in case. No point in getting rusty, gathering dust in total celibacy, even if this didn't look like a proper run out.

He gave the impression, he decided, that he worked in the theatre, but not camp. Intellectual. Creative. Which, of course, he was. Eyes a trifle manic, perhaps. He supposed it was part of his charisma that he should be alone, that he was not, in common with most men of his age, totally taken up with mowing the lawn, and worrying that his kids might be having a sex life.

The divorce, now well into the past, was beginning to feel more glamorous, less a failure. He was apprehensive that tonight Dodo might feel it something they had in common.

He wondered if the woman he'd bumped into outside the house would be at the party. She might well live in the area.

It really was quite extraordinary. She walked round the corner, and then her hair exploded. Suddenly. For a moment, her head was surrounded with chestnut fire. She stood, laughing up at the sky. In a second, all was normal again.

As she walked towards him, purposeful, but looking down, he wondered why he'd not stepped aside. Instead, he stood still, and let her bump against his shoulder.

She jumped aside, startled, catching at her hair with one hand, trying to restrain the wild energy of it. Everything else, the wicker shopping basket, the long, straight damson coat, was so conventional.

He opened the bathroom window, which was on the front of the house, and looked down into the street below. It happened there, outside the gate. It had seemed unavoidable. To be unavoidable suggested fate. As an atheist, he didn't think the stars influenced the tides of life. But it might be possible, scientifically, that the moon, which once swirled the waters in and around our ancestral cells, might still call man to the echo of celestial movement, should we wish to follow.

It was difficult to forget that hair, but the woman would have no reason to remember him. Nothing to remind her of the small joke which existed without words, an ephemeral span, frail as a half-made cobweb.

'You're a fool,' said Lex, and slammed the window shut.

# Chapter Four

'We needn't stay long,' said Fenn, as they walked down Springfield Lane, towards the party in Dodo's flat. She walked between her husband and sister, arming them along, both reluctant for different reasons. Hughie hated all parties. 'I'm a person's person,' he was fond of saying, 'I'm not one of the herd.'

'I shall help with the washing-up if no-one speaks to me,' said Pru. When social opportunity loomed, excitement evaporated, and fear of failure hung over her. She'd washed her hair especially, and it had gone wispy on her. She wondered if there would be any men there on their own.

Springfield Lane was the remains of a village. All over England are such remnants of village streets, hidden, disguised, absorbed into towns. Springfield Lane had been a group of Victorian houses grown up round a much older church. The big house, Mellowstones, was up for sale. The older cottages had disappeared when the fields had gone, eaten up by urban growth. The well-spaced Victorian buildings had been sown with catch crops of bungalows. The invisible time threads of community had been broken, but replaced by other links; instead of the routines of the church, and the farming seasons in the lost fields, there were neighbourhood-watch schemes, and coffee mornings among the unemployed.

Fenn's relationship with Dodo went back to school-days, but would never have been sustained, had they not been held together by the bonding quality of the Lane. They had always been different.

Fenn was always the conventional one, the con-former. It was Dodo who was the first girl in the class to lose her virginity. She smoked small cheroots in her twenties, claiming that cannabis were fattening. Recently, she worked on a telephone chatline, the sort the government banned later in the year, because of public indignation. When she confided to Fenn that she found the work overstimulating, Fenn insisted she packed it in.

Fenn had married kindly Hughie. Dodo had married a flamboyant womanizer. She was over her bad patch now, which had come when her husband, whom she'd always referred to as that stingy bugger, had walked out one Thursday morning. Dodo had been surprisingly upset, and spent some effort on trying to lure him back, unfortunately to no effect, since he had found a much younger, and totally liberated version of Dodo.

Dodo had since put her effort into finding herself, and becoming more interesting, with dubious results.

'Dodo's friends are always into welfare,' said Hughie. 'Though it's difficult to know whether they're in it, or on it.'

Dodo opened the door. She wore a long brown dress, making her look, Pru thought, like a polystyrene rugby ball. She clasped a collection of Celtic chains and pendants to her midriff. Her hair, which was abundantly curly, the circular whirls perfectly echoing the shape of her face, was restrained by a bandeau across the brow.

Hughie winced, and was reminded of John McEnroe in his early days. He'd never liked headbands since.

'Sherry?' said Dodo. She giggled hopefully. The

sherry was once dark, sweet and cheap. Now, diluted, it appeared, while still in the glass, to be dry and expensive. 'Circulate,' she whispered. 'I can't stay. The rice is in crisis.' She bounced off in multi vapours of scent, moisturizer and hairspray.

Dodo's sitting-room looked better full of people. A crowd obscured the collections; the shelf of dolls from France, the canal jugs and buckets, the Dove Cottage teapot, the Islamic prayer mat on the wall, and the screen pinned with postcards, curling with dehydration. It wasn't easy to feel serene in Dodo's sitting-room.

A woman wearing metal-rimmed specs on a chain, and a beige cardigan afflicted by wool lag, came over to Fenn. 'What do you DO?' She asked, zooming in close to Fenn's face.

'I run a small catering . . .'

'I chair the committee for furthering the insect life of Moor Park, as well the experimental group for method acting, and members' own plays.' She looked closely at Fenn for signs of envy, and finding none, gazed round for someone interesting to talk at. Spotting a man with a squint, and a scarlet tie, she moved over to him. She progressed by heaving her shoulders round fellow guests, the rest following.

'She looks like colonic irrigation to me,' said Fenn. 'I'd better rescue Dodo in the kitchen. It'll be chaos by now.'

'Where's Marie going?' Fenn noticed Dodo's daughter, in a drooping patchwork leather anorak, making for the door. Fenn was relying on Marie looking after Damaris in Australia. Marie was sensible.

'Out to feed the homeless,' said Dodo. 'Would you believe? I mean she can't fancy the Vicar. Hell. Look at that rice.'

'Almost beyond recall,' said Fenn, wincing, as she assessed the saucepan.

*　　*　　*

As Marie walked out of the door, Lex walked in. He was momentarily still, his head slightly tipped back so that he could look down the length of his masculine nose. In the subdued light, he looked swarthy, and his hair very black, none of the grey showing. His eyelids were moodily heavy, or so they looked to Dodo, who had abandoned the rice to Fenn, and was keeping an eye out from the kitchen. He's feeling sexy, Dodo thought, even decadent, and went over.

'Join the madhouse.' Dodo, once more, clasped the fistful of Celtic art to herself, to stop it bouncing alarmingly and noisily off her chest as she walked.

'A mature gathering,' said Lex, noting there were no women younger than himself, and most of the men were the type who wore socks with sandals, though as it was winter, there was no proof they did. Coming here was a mistake, it confirmed he was almost middle-aged himself.

'Ripeness is all,' whispered Dodo, lowering her voice to a sexy murmur. 'There are no mindless tarts here, if that's what you mean.' She gave him a little derisory smile. 'We're all quite grown up. I've got to do the hostess bit now. We can have a nice little chat, all about you, later.' She leaned, momentarily, comfortingly, on his arm, to let the musk oil get up his nostrils, before dashing back to the kitchen.

Lex shuddered. The only person he recognized was the old girl from the downstairs flat, May someone. He'd seen her at the window, staring out. He'd do the polite thing, and then escape.

May was, at that moment, talking to Pru, who noted the scornful eyes, the casual swagger, as Lex came up to them. Pru thought he looked what you'd call a nasty piece of work, and big headed with it.

'Lex. From the upstairs flat.' He smiled at the two

women, one reduced by the years, the other diminished by disappointment.

May didn't seem able to get her mind round this introduction. She expected a full name.

Pru chipped in helpfully. 'Pru. Not local. May and I were making plans for church in the morning. Do you worship round here, Lex?' Deliberately using a person's name was a tip Pru had mistakenly been given, for getting on well at parties. It was supposed to show genuine interest. Strangely, it seemed to irritate some people.

'I'm an atheist.'

'That's sad,' said Pru, thinking it explained a lot.

'Probably laziness,' said May. 'Never given your mind over to it.'

'I can't take the Resurrection.' Lex raised one questioning eyebrow. This was a dumb moment to start a proper conversation.

'You don't have to take it. It's given,' said May briskly. She smiled at him, because it seemed civil.

Her nose seemed to wobble alarmingly. She had no laughter lines in her face, as if the smile were only a rare treat. Her eyes were dark brown and bright with little white showing, the sort you see on cheap teddy bears. Lex smiled back.

'Because it's hard to understand, you don't have to reject it.' May might be getting a little forgetful, but on some subjects she was as firm as Peter's rock.

'It's not the metaphysics I find difficult,' said Lex. 'It's the variety. Which version do you favour? One, two or three witnesses? Do you want the guards to be there? Angels inside the tomb, or outside? There are limitations, of course. If you want Salome as a witness, then you only get one angel. If you have Mary Magdalene on her own, you get two angels and the popular quote.'

'At least you know your Bible, but I don't like your

35

mocking tone.' May began to fumble with her evening bag. She might be right, but felt unlikely to win the argument against Lex, him being so cocky.

'It's easy to scoff, Lex,' said Pru, and she put her arm round May, protectively. 'Just because you have no faith.'

'According to Mark, Pilate was surprised that Jesus died so quickly. Perhaps he was never dead? Did you read that case in the paper last week, where a woman in Leicester sat up in the hospital morgue, and asked for a cigarette?'

'Anyway,' said May, with a hint of triumph, 'what happens in Leicester isn't in the Gospels, is it?' She walked away, and took refuge in the kitchen.

The kitchen was taller than it was long, with a small modern window, now totally steamed up. Kitchens are always a problem when a bedroom floor is converted into a flat. It didn't help that the wallpaper's red fish swam in every direction. Fenn wiped down the draining area, because it didn't look wholesome.

May sat at the table, very upright, mopping her face with the tea towel. 'Have a tissue,' said Dodo. 'It's more hygienic. Whatever's the matter with you?'

'Nothing.'

'Then why are you crying?' asked Fenn, taking the tea towel away, and pulling out a generous bunch of peach tissues from a floral tissue box holder.

'I'm just having a little rest. On my own.'

'I saw you talking to Lex,' said Dodo.

'He's not my type of person,' said May. 'Not at all.'

'But sexy.' Dodo gazed down into the saucepan. The rice, peppers and the scattering of prawns of the paella had united into an impervious block. Each breath of steam brought the union closer. She put the pan on the draining board and tried to add back water. The union hissed spitefully and only the least tenacious grains of rice fell back, and floated untemptingly in the grey liquid.

The sole reason for the giving of the party was to provide opportunity in the Lex area. It was difficult to make progress speaking only on the stairs. With hindsight, it had been a mistake to suggest he paid the rent by direct debit. Now, the guests were failing to sparkle, May was blubbing all over the salad, and the star dish had turned against her.

'I should have put up a better defence. But he was so . . . ruthless. So sarcastic,' May said, thinking that Lewis had never been cruel like that, though he would have argued on just the same lines. He'd been very naughty about God.

Dodo poured a whisky, and another for May, then sat cross-legged on the kitchen floor breathing calmly and slowly, eyes closed.

'I'm feeling very calm. I'm very calm indeed. I recognize the problem, and let it slip away from me on the water, glide away on the stream. I stay very calm. Quiet. Very calm and quiet. Shall I go and get more drink? Stop them noticing the food?'

'Pull yourself together,' said Fenn. 'We'll put some wine into that mess.'

'Wine's an antiseptic,' said May.

Fenn sloshed in most of a bottle of hock, and thickened it with butter and flour. She found cardamom and mace in the recesses of a cupboard, leftovers from a cookery nightschool. She seasoned, added lime juice, and love.

'It's not exactly paella,' said Dodo. Her forehead was moist with the steam, and she flapped her arms, like a hen, to dispel the stickiness the tension was creating.

'It's an improvement,' said Fenn. 'Serve it before anything else goes wrong.'

'It's a miracle, Fenn.'

'I know.'

Dodo looked out of her kitchen at her party rotating and gurgling in her sitting-room, and sighed with pleasure now that the crisis was over. She loved parties, loved the sensation of warmth and friendship she got from a gathering up of friends.

'Twelfth Night,' she giggled to Fenn, 'is the ideal time. People have just about got their livers back in shape after New Year's eve, though I think some of them might have made more effort with their appearance.'

'Saturnalia,' said Fenn, recognizing the heartwarming orgy in the cold grip of winter, dancing flames like an oasis of warmth, in the snow. 'It was there long before Christmas, and even then it was a time of hope, a yearning that new life would come to the world.'

'Fenn, how could you?' said May. 'You sound like the Bishop of Durham, pretending Christmas isn't there.'

'Well,' said Fenn, and left it at that. 'I'd better see that Pru is OK. Oh, there you are Hughie.'

'Let's find you a nice place to sit, May,' said Hughie, and led her away, carrying her plate with its transiently perfect rice, two prawns, and a leaf of lambs lettuce. He saw the kitchen was no place for him.

Lex was bored, and being attacked by the woman in the woolly cardigan. Dodo couldn't remember who she was, but forced a plate into her hands, to quieten her down. 'Perhaps you could help me,' she said to Lex.

Grateful to be rescued, he absent-mindedly rubbed his thumb on Dodo's plump shoulder. Dodo, pleased, moved slightly closer. Her body language was wasted.

Lex turned his head, and stared across the room, not at all absent-mindedly, and certainly not bored. He was looking at Fenn Meadowcroft. She was leaning against the kitchen door post, arms crossed, head tilted back, contemplating the party, as it ate the rice. Her dark auburn hair was mostly up, with a few tendrils escaping down the back of her neck. The colour was enhanced by an indigo silk shirt. She seemed set apart from the bustle, from the frantic conversations, from the collective party instinct of the rest of Dodo's friends, all hell-bent on being interesting. Lex watched her move away, half smiling, to talk to the dreadful little spinster with the religious hang up.

'You must know where there's a party,' said Damaris. 'You know everyone round here. You can't have a decent local social life if you've been posted off to an institution, like I was. All the people I know are miles away.' She was beginning to have serious doubts as to whether Marie was the best person to go to Australia with. It was with both having to do autumn A-level retakes that they were drawn together. That had been a waste of time too. She dreaded the results coming.

'I said I'd help at the soup kitchen. It was really worthwhile at Christmas. It's awful out there being homeless,' said Marie. 'I promised.'

'Why did you bother to come round then?'

'To see if you were all right.'

'I could have gone to a party in Clapham. Everyone will be there, but Popkin found out Ed was expelled for smoking a bit of grass.'

'You can help me with the soup if you like. It's turkey. The Vicar made a request for carcasses.'

'Jesus,' said Damaris.

'Is the rice edible, Pru?' Fenn was trying to find a man for Pru to meet.

'Rather good. Look out. A dreadful person's coming over. He was so nasty to poor May.'

'*Ananas au cointreau gelée*,' Lex said, and twirled

the plate round like a fancy waiter. The jelly, of fragile nature despite three hours in the fridge set as low as it would go, slurped into a formless mass. But it was enough for an excuse.

'We meet again,' he said to Fenn. 'A peace offering for being clumsy?'

Fenn didn't speak, as the rice was beginning to take its revenge, and was difficult to swallow, but she couldn't stop her smile. He was a funny man.

'A French recipe?' ventured Pru, determined to forgive, and noticing Lex had lost his arrogant sneer.

'Tinned pineapple in packet jelly with a teaspoonful of liquor essence, I imagine.' He gave the second plate to Pru.

'I hoped it was French. I go to the most fascinating French classes. Do you go to classes at all, Lex?'

'All day. I teach. Well, intermittently. On supply at the moment. Plenty of change. Start somewhere new on Monday.'

'That's interesting,' said Pru.

'I was miles away this morning,' said Fenn, swallowing at last, surprised he should be a teacher.

'I know.'

The low protein content of the meal made the conversation aggressive. There were unstructured discussions on Freud, aromatherapy and gay marriages. As well as people from meditation classes, painting, Weight Watchers and the Alternative Health group, there were friends from the office. Dodo, after giving up the telephone chatline, worked part-time for a company who set up exhibitions for artists devoid of talent, to sell to people, who knew nothing about pictures. Such friends did not waste their time talking about golf, holidays or children. They'd rejected the establishment, and were looking for something enviable to put in its place.

Fenn found a corner to sit with her coffee, by a pyramid of fir branches, which pretended to be a Christmas tree. She tried to shrug off the hassle of the day. Pru was sitting on the sofa with May, and a man in a black shirt and white kipper tie, all of them looking hopeful. Hughie was out of sight. Fenn suspected that he'd found refuge in the loo. When last seen he was being seriously mauled by Woolly Cardigan.

She also tried to shrug off the effect of talking to Lex, this strange feeling of wanting to smile, to laugh for no reason. It must only have been charm, this impression of interest which he gave, just easy charm. When the pudding was finished, she went into the kitchen, to allow him to escape.

Fenn, nevertheless, wasn't surprised when he came over again, and sat on the floor beside her.

'I'm in provocative mood.' He leaned back against the wall, and smiled questioningly up at her.

'I know. You were unkind to May. Religion is her staff.'

'One should be controversial. It's one's duty. People accept things too easily. Truth is not set in stone. "What's to come is still unsure." You see, Shakespeare's just as good as the Bible for quotes.'

'*Twelfth Night*,' said Fenn, pleased she could show him she recognized it.

He nodded slowly, looking at her, trying to get her in an eye lock.

Fenn took refuge where she could. 'So you teach English?' she asked lightly, giving her coffee an extra stir.

'Yes. I'm stuck with that. Quite enjoy it.' Lex moved about, trying to sit comfortably. '*Twelfth Night* is a sad play. The fool, you know. "For the rain it raineth every day".'

Fenn saw now Lex wasn't as young as she'd thought;

41

he might be almost her own age. He was also more attractive than most men who she met through Hughie, or through her own friends. Wives like herself didn't have friends of their own, who were men, she realized.

'Are you never happy?' she asked.

'I was happy B.R.'

'What's British Rail got to do with it?'

'B.R. Before Rebecca.' Lex looked enigmatically into his glass. 'I created her, you see, but of course at the time, I thought she was real. It's called love.'

'What happened A.R.?'

'She went to Canada. After the divorce. I nourished the dream. I created Eve before she was into apples, and the Mona Lisa without the smirk.' Lex gazed at her, full of gratitude. Fenn thought, he's going to say he's never told anyone else all this before.

'Of course, I tell everyone,' said Lex, stretching his legs with the pleasure of a cat. 'Every woman. It's interesting to see how they react. They're sympathetic, or encouraging. Then they seduce me. Occasionally. Well, one did once. Almost.'

The soup was beginning to cool. Damaris wondered what they would think at St Hilary's if they could see her now. Well, they never would. Though, of course, it could be turned to advantage. It had novelty appeal, that's for sure. She watched Marie spoon up a full cup.

'There you go, Mavis.'

The khaki mittens over blue fingers curled round the cup, warming the hands first.

'You know their names?' Damaris said.

'Some of them. Mavis is a regular.'

'Got some bread to go with that, Mavis,' said a youth who Damaris had only just noticed. His face was sandwiched between a brown woolly hat and grey scarf. He gave Mavis a croissant, leftovers from the Pot Pourri coffee shop. 'Now don't be choosy about it,' he said quietly. He smiled down at her, waiting for a tiny, friendly response.

Marie smiled, tenderly watching Mavis slurp up her turkey soup. 'Why don't you hand the rest of those round, Murray?' she said.

Damaris stopped stirring the soup; she'd been thinking about the party in Clapham. Now she watched the boy. Murray. His eyes were fairly small, but his mouth was full, and rather damp looking.

Hughie emerged from the loo, where he had taken sanctuary with the *Times Literary Supplement* which, with forethought, he had brought with him. Unfortunately, the queue outside was growing restive.

Knowing he must make one gesture at least of communing with these unlikable people, he proffered his one funny story, that of the Bombay taxi driver. Dodo's friends, avid for evidence of racism, gathered round him.

Fenn and Lex were outside the circle of the party, within their own patch of ease. 'Do you find it difficult to be honest with yourself?' she asked.

'Do you think I'm honest?'

'I don't think you're as sad as you make out.'

'Absolutely right. I'm lucky. Forever chased by panting women, especially nymphos like Dodo.'

'Yes?'

Lex began to laugh, closing his eyes. He opened them again to look at her. 'We should have this discussion all over again. When?'

'When?' Fenn was questioning the word, not the time, and pretended to take a sip out of her empty coffee cup. The circle of ease was gone.

'Tomorrow? "I am slain by a fair cruel maid".'

'Is *Twelfth Night* the only play you quote from?'

43

'Tonight, yes. And only the Fool, you observe. The wisest man in the play. I empathize with him totally. You haven't answered my question.'

Hughie's flurry of social activity attracted Dodo. Her face was slightly shining in the low light, and she leaned towards Hughie, so that now and again, very gently, very casually, her chest brushed against him. He could feel her through the *Times Literary Supplement* tucked in the inside pocket of his jacket.

'Dodo's a happy woman,' said Fenn. 'She has her moments. This looks like one of them. Hughie's getting wary. I know that look. I think he wants rescuing.'

Lex was not to be lost. 'You haven't answered the question.' Fenn knew he was still looking at her, but she refused to look back into his face. It would be like touching.

Hughie made his escape from Dodo, and came over. 'Been having a jolly time, old thing?' He was beginning to sound gregarious, as it was nearly time to leave.

May and Pru appeared. May whispered, 'Time to go. Would Dodo call me a cab, do you think?'

Hugh took her arm and said, 'We'll see you home. No need for a cab tonight.'

Pru giggled. 'Doesn't Dodo give good parties. I've been talking all evening. George, over there with a beard, is a sex therapist. He was very interesting. And I met Harold who has, surprisingly, spent some time in prison. So amusing about it too.'

'I can't compete with that, I'm afraid. Can you?' Hughie said to Lex. 'I'm just a simple English teacher.'

'Snap.'

'It's harder than sex therapy,' mused Hughie. 'Getting anything into their heads.'

'Not my problem,' said Lex. 'Never give them answers. Make them ask the right questions.'

'Heady stuff. Dangerous. Could end up knowing nothing. Where are you?'

'I'm on supply at the moment. Going to some private dump next term. I'm told they live in the ark.'

'I work at the best private school in this area. We have an excellent reputation. I assume it's not St Anthony's?'

'Thank you for our conversation,' said Fenn to Lex, and led Hughie firmly away. St Anthony's was the best private school in the area simply because it was the only private school.

'What did you make of Lex?' Dodo whispered to Fenn when she fetched her coat from Dodo's bedroom.

'Enigmatic.'

'You don't think he's a bit camp? I keep looking at the way he walks. Seems perfectly normal.'

'You can never tell.'

'I intend to find out. The value of celibacy lies in self-discipline, and you can't practise self-discipline without opportunity. It's like fasting in an empty pantry.' Dodo stood before her mirror, and ran her hands down her flanks, minimizing them in her mind's eye.

Damaris got home before her parents. Who would have thought it? Not a wasted evening after all. Yes, she would have to use Marie to find out about this bloke, Murray. Rather quiet, but intriguing. He looked terribly serious. What he needed was to be woken up about himself. Damaris knew all about that. She'd woken up quite a few of the sixth form boys last term.

She opened the window, and had a quick cig in the fresh air. Mother was a prig about smoking. The air was a bit damp, and didn't feel like winter at all.

From the depths of a suede boot in the wardrobe she extracted a bottle of South African sherry and had a comforting three swigs.

\*     \*     \*

'You look shattered,' Dodo said to Lex when she had seen the last person out. 'You need a decent drink.'

'I'm afraid I've upset every guest I've spoken to. There's someone I want to ask . . .'

'I won't be a moment.' Dodo wanted to freshen up for the next phase.

Marie came in and found Lex, leaning against the window frame, staring out into the street, across the front garden.

'Have you had a horrid time, Lex?'

'Hello, Marie. No, actually I've had a fascinating evening. You been to a party?'

She shook her head. 'We took the soup to the usual places. I thought it would be like any other night. It was worse, of course, more drunks than usual. You know, they really feel a hope now that Christmas is over that things will get better. And, of course, they don't. It's so sad. What was so fascinating?'

'I was going to ask your mother about someone. But that mayn't be too clever. I think I'd better go. I'll let myself out.'

Marie went to her own room. Warmed by her father's left behind anorak, she put her pillow longways up, and wrote her journal on her knee. She had used the anorak ever since he left as a winter dressing gown.

She wrote, 'Mum is feeling randy again. I can always tell. I do hope she doesn't try to seduce Lex. He might prove reluctant, and then she'd be hurt. Dearest Mum, she's shown so much spirit, ever since Daddy went away. Tonight we fed forty-seven people.' She put out the light and lay down.

Hughie unlocked the door of May's ground floor flat, and switched on the hall light for her. He waited until she seemed fully orientated before leaving. The lapse about the taxi was forgotten.

Outside, the damp night air felt like spring. Hughie thought how nice Fenn looked tonight. He shuddered at the memory of Dodo leaning against him, and squeezed Fenn's arm.

'I always feel shy at parties,' said Fenn, and looked at Hughie, hopefully. 'Did I look . . . you know . . . OK tonight?'

'Fine,' said Hughie. 'You don't think that dreadful man is coming to St Anthony's do you? Woodhouse must have recovered from his breakdown by now.'

'Lex is very intelligent. Why do you call him dreadful?'

'Rum ideas about teaching. Why's his hair short at the front, and all over his collar at the back?' Hughie didn't like the way Lex was sitting in a corner with Fenn, as Hughie saw them, as soon as he was forced out of the loo.

Fenn lifted up her face to the clement night, and realized she didn't mind that Hughie, once again, failed to reassure her. She could afford to feel happy with Hughie because, at this moment, she felt good about herself, complete, not looking for something new. She'd enjoyed talking to Lex, but that was that.

Hughie was a fixed point. It was comforting that he produced no disconcerting surprises. You knew where you were with Hughie. He never wavered from his routines. He was just as perfectly predictable in bed. No squirming, no animal grunts, just a comfortingly familiar, localized explosion. That was Hughie. Fenn was content that new fields in that area were not for her.

Ahead of them Pru walked in the darkness, reliving her social whirl, wondering, why, as always, there was nothing that would come to anything. Nothing had happened that would bring her eventual happiness, the sort of reward promised by the Lord to those who had faith.

In the dark bedroom, May lay flat on her back, straight, hand lightly folded across her stomach. Parties were a terrible strain. Shouting, not talking. People drinking too much. Children's parties were the worst of all. Little Rose's parties, my, they were hard work. But worth it just to see her happy face.

May switched the light back on, and sat up in bed. She could never sleep after a party, the mind still raced. Perhaps she'd drunk a little too much, but they were all such tedious people. She had to laugh at that Lex, thinking he'd upset her. How could he know that all he'd done was make her think of Lewis again. Ever since she'd climbed into bed an hour ago, she'd gone over their arguments, the ones she'd won, the ones she'd lost.

I could read for a while, she mused, or I could write a letter. Slowly, she climbed out of bed, and got a writing pad from the sitting room. Letters, so many letters she'd written to Lewis. She wished now that she hadn't burned his to her when she married Tom. It had seemed the fair thing to do.

She wrote carefully, she loved writing to people. In some ways it was the easiest way of talking to them.

In her bedroom, Dodo experimented with the lengths of her bra straps, endeavouring to minimize her prow. They flattened out a bit when low slung, but that made her look dumpy. Strung up she looked tarty. 'Sod them,' she said, and comforted herself by smelling the skin of her arm. It was still rich from the bath oil, a strong brew of musk and sandalwood, well seeped into every inch, making her feel silken and as soft as double cream. It was a long time since the divorce, time she began to live again. Time, also, that she found a better provider than the last one.

From her scarf drawer she pulled out a crumpled piece of paper, her biorhythm chart for a whole year, an offer made in the *Sunday Popular*. She checked on what she already knew. Yes, she was on a triple optimum, at her peak in all three areas, physical, mental and emotional. She did seven deep breaths, the magical number, stressing exhalation, to relax her face muscles, and brushed her lips with non-greasy salve.

Carrying the whisky bottle from the vegetable rack, and picking up clean glasses, she was ready. 'Lex,' she called. 'Here I am. Lex?'

The sitting room was empty. She looked optimistically into the bedroom, checked that the bathroom was free, then sat down on the sofa, breathing in the smells of the spent party, smoke and booze and cheap scent. 'Sod men, sod the lot of them,' she said, and filled the tumbler to the brim.

# Chapter Five

Fenn's kitchen was large, the old coal house and outside loo areas having been incorporated into it. At the hall door end was a sofa, very old, with a saggy, neutral linen loose cover. It was a place for contemplation and recovery. By the side window, which overlooked a paved patio and the path to the back door, was her computer. It sat on a table stained dark green, and her print-out files were covered in a russet hessian, so none of it looked so very out of place against the pale oak dresser, and the large pine table. There was always a lingering smell of toast, or of mint, or sometimes, of shortbread; this kitchen was not a room to let go lightly of its pleasures.

Fenn put coffee mugs on the table. Hughie was in his study, pleased to have survived the party, looking forward to the preparation of the War Poets course, and wondering if it would be entirely fair to gloss over some of their left-wing ideas. Not so much gloss over, of course, but shift the emphasis to use of language, and so on.

'Pru,' Fenn called. 'Coffee.' She checked her computerized recipe file for ingredients which she would need for the business lunch on Thursday, and decided to run a new print out. The soup section, particularly, was getting ragged and untidy.

Outside the second kitchen window, overlooking the garden, the sky was watery and cool, breathless for the spring still far off. 'Dear God, bless Pru, and help her to find someone. She needs to be married, in order to flower. Doesn't she?' The grey veils moved slowly across the face of God, enigmatic and deaf.

Pru came slowly down the stairs. She seemed always to move close to the wall.

'Here you are. Toast?'

'Just a wafer.'

Pru put her own slice of wholegrain in the toaster, and watched it expectantly, until the toast jerked up. She found sadly, the grains were burned and the substance was pale. Paradoxically, it smelled charred, yet remained undercooked.

The back door opened, and Dodo erupted through it, prominent in a billowing cerise shirt, not tucked in. Dodo never confronted her waistline by trying to define it. She'd been extravagant with the musk body spray.

'Well,' she said. 'Postmortem? Did it go well, or didn't it?'

'You got through a lot of rice,' said Pru, smearing her toast with polyunsaturates, annoyed that Dodo had not thanked her for doing some washing up.

'OK, the food was patchy, but parties are for people. PEOPLE, for heaven's sake. At a proper party you simply don't notice the food because of scintillating conversation out of great minds.'

'The woman in a woolly cardigan didn't have a great mind.'

'No, well, poor Cynthia was only there to take up space. I'm thinking of the characters. Lex, for one. So original.'

Fenn weighed flour for the Yorkshire pudding. Four ounces. She paused. What was Dodo up to? Had she noticed the quiet conversation in the corner? Fenn measured the milk into a jug. 'I hope he doesn't turn up at St Anthony's.' She paid close attention to the egg as it flopped into the milk, wiping a white globule off her wrist. 'Hughie will react.'

'I don't suppose you spoke to Lex?' Dodo said to Pru.

'I spoke to so many people,' said Pru. 'Including him. Nasty little toad.'

Dodo smiled round, and took Fenn's coffee, fortifying it with extra sugar. 'Actually, Lex is not quite my type. But he's useful in a lull.'

'Was he useful last night?' enquired Pru, wondering if this meant putting the hoover over the carpet, or something else.

'Not really. I was pretty tired anyway.'

'We are going to church, aren't we?' said Pru.

The liquidizer compelled the eggs and flour into a marriage, a batter, with the power to engage, later, with heat, and emerge as a miracle.

After another noisy slurp of coffee, Dodo took a letter from her handbag. 'Got to post this for May.' She held it against the steam coming from the coffee filter, watching the flap get soggy, and detach.

'Dodo?'

'It's the address. It's where she lived as a child. I'm certain those houses aren't there now.'

'They might be. Leave it alone, Dodo.'

Dodo pulled the letter from its envelope. '"My dear Rose"' she read, and looked at Fenn. 'Rose was the child that died, wasn't she? Listen to this. "How are my little grandchildren today? It was so lovely to spend Christmas with you. I had such fun choosing the doll. I found it in a shop in Kensington High Street. And the soldiers for little Thomas. I know his grandfather had some just like it when he was a boy . . ."'

Slowly, Dodo put the letter back in the envelope, and

tried to stick the flap down again. 'I'm sorry,' she said. 'I should never have done that. I'm sorry.'

'She's gaga,' said Pru.

'No,' said Fenn. 'There's nothing wrong with May. Dreams and reality have got interchanged. May's fine.'

'Quite,' said Dodo. 'For the time being. I don't want the worry of who will be in that bottom flat, do I?'

Damaris wafted into the kitchen, in a towelling dressing gown, which she'd pulled out of the dirty linen basket. 'Coffee. Black. Black. Black.' She ran herself a glass of water. 'No thank you, Pru. I don't know how anyone can eat in the mornings.' She thumped on the radio. 'Hell. Why's it on Classic FM?' Her right eye still had a crunchy particle of leftover sleep in the corner. Before she could tune into Radio One, and turn up the volume, headlines cut through the room.

'It has been confirmed that five people, all British, have been killed when a light aircraft flying from Marseilles to Luton was forced to make an emergency landing over the Kent coast. Within seconds of touching down, the plane was engulfed in flame, although the emergency services were on hand. The sole survivor is a child of eight, thrown clear before the fire took its toll. He is believed to be called Simeon, and that his parents and two sisters are victims of the crash.'

Damaris switched the radio off.

'Dear God,' said Pru, and bowed her head.

Fenn stared out of the window, at the moving clouds with accusing eyes. 'Why are we kinder than God?' she asked. 'Somebody tell me that.'

'He must have his reasons,' whispered Pru.

Damaris lay her head on the table. 'I've got a filthy headache,' she said.

'Are you hung over?' demanded Fenn.

'Suppose so.' Damaris was whiter than usual.

'Sit up,' said Fenn, her voice raised. 'Drink your coffee. Then get washed. It's your own stupid fault. Think of that child on the plane. What's he done to deserve that?'

'It's the airline, not poor Damaris, you should be shouting at,' said Dodo.

'May God bless that poor child,' said Pru.

'Why should God bless him now,' demanded Fenn, 'when it was God who let it happen in the first place?' In her mind, the child, Simeon, stood beside Ray, locked in his black world in a bed in Adelaide, and with all the other people, whose suffering was longer than a mere three hours, but were never, seemingly, touched by the love of God.

'Calm down. There's nothing any of us can do.' Dodo gave herself a second spoon of sugar, for comfort.

A figure passed the side window, coming from the back gate.

'It's Doug,' said Fenn. 'Why's he here on a Sunday?' She opened the door, calm again. Doug was not someone that one could afford to appear flurried before. She tried, by force of personality, to stop him coming in. He walked straight past her, instinctively challenged by her hostility. His haunches, in tight, black leather, were as robust as those of an ageing stallion.

'Me filofax. Left it in the duster trug.' Doug opened the cupboard, and retrieved the diary from among the tins of polish and bottles of cleaner. He leered round triumphantly, sensing the unease in the room, as Pru took in the ponytail, the small red mouth within the seedlings of a beard, and the triangle of white flesh, where his shirt divided at the point of greatest circumference.

'Doug cleans on Monday and Friday mornings,' explained Fenn, catching Pru's expression, who was clearly wondering if he were a friend. 'Doug's taken the place of Mrs Gladoby.' Fenn failed to sound as enthusiastic about the new arrangement as she'd intended.

'Vroom Enterprises,' said Doug. 'Mrs M is extremely lucky that she's got the boss come in. I could send one of the boys.' His tone and sneer suggested her luck might soon run out.

Dodo looked at the breadth of his back. The jacket was expensive.

'You must be busy, needing your filofax so urgently,' said Fenn, trying to shepherd him to the door.

'I thought you'd like to know something else.' Doug looked round triumphantly, like a cat that's felled a pigeon. 'Murray's got a place at Oxford.'

Damaris put down her mug of coffee on top of Pru's toast.

'The Poly, I presume,' said Dodo, 'though I know they all pretend to be universities these days.'

'Balliol.'

'Christ,' said Dodo.

'Balliol,' said Doug. 'Ma's delighted. Took a day off the stall yesterday, to celebrate. Says brains will out. Shall I see you in church?'

'In church?'

'I'm popping in to see how Murray looked in his robes.'

'I noticed at Christmas there was a new youth in the choir.'

'Wished I'd got him in as a little 'un, his voice has broken now, of course. But he's a good little singer. They wanted some more tenors.'

'I didn't realize you were religious,' said Fenn.

'I'm not. But he'll meet the right people there. Go a bit upmarket. Mind you, I told him to look out for the Vicar. You get a lot of poufters in that trade you know.'

'The Vicar is a married man. I know his wife.'

'Doesn't mean a thing. Flowers and berries on the same twig these days.'

Doug shoved the trug back into the cupboard. With a confident smile round the kitchen, he swung out of the door, leaving behind a faint trace of incense, and Fenn scowling.

'Dreadful man,' said Pru. 'What's the world coming to with Doug's type of person going to university. Do you think he's telling the truth?'

'He did say Murray, didn't he?' asked Damaris, her head off the table now.

'Precisely. What a jumped-up name for a person of his class,' said Dodo.

'I know for a fact his mother smokes cannabis,' said Fenn, 'been in court for possession.'

She poured the slinky Yorkshire pudding batter into a yellow basin and covered it with a clean tea towel. There, out of sight, the gluten softened and changed state. It became open to change, aware that flour and eggs are not fixed and forever the same. What it could not know is that the miracle of the Yorkshire pudding, like all miracles, is more rarely seen now than in the past.

From his bathroom window, which he'd opened to let out the steam from the shower, Lex watched the small group come down Springfield Lane. When they came level, May came out and joined them. Lex watched unseen, and confirmed his impressions. Hughie, dull and kind, was being especially courteous to May, frail as a lost sparrow. Dodo, who must have left the house earlier, came in to collect a coat. She walked with a substantial bounce.

Fenn came into sight. Her shoulders swayed energetically as she strode along. She looked almost angry. Her hair was tucked up today, under a velvet Paddington bear hat. Lex didn't even notice Pru. At the last minute, Damaris rushed out after them. Then, amazingly, Fenn glanced up at his window. He smiled. He deliberately made it a mocking smile. Cool, no trace of anxiety. She glanced away, without any response, as if she'd never seen him.

Fenn looked straight ahead. She was, in fact, thrown at the sight of Lex's bare shoulders, not too certain that he would be wearing anything at all, out of vision, below the sill.

Damaris wrinkled her nose at the smell of dust within the church, and that of stale candles. She'd not come to St Theodosia's since her confirmation. The then Vicar, during her preparation, said, 'You must have heard of the Atonement.' Damaris explained it put humankind at a disadvantage to have been sacrificed for, then for ever expected to be grateful. The Vicar went on to say that Damaris was exactly the sort of person for whom our Lord died, appearing to accept her argument, while remaining in a pout of total disapproval. Damaris only went through with the charade to please Hughie.

Fenn looked round her, lifting her face to the Easter window. All the figures wore shades of cream and its shadows were the blue of cool places. There were narcissi growing by the entrance to the tomb, and green jars of spices scattered on the ground. She had always taken comfort from that window, from its beauty, from its timeless hope.

Fenn had accepted what she'd been told, wanting it to be true, the comfort of believing there were saving hands. Today, she saw this information belonged to her childhood, no more true than Father Christmas, or fairies. Ray was the truth. Ray and Simeon. She was no more a child, but it took courage to be grown up.

*     *     *

'And so we pray,' said William, 'for all those who have lost their lives in the terrible air disaster on the news this morning. We pray that God may give his peace to those who rest now, upon another, and more tranquil shore. Let us pray especially for little Simeon, who has survived the crash but at the terrible price of losing his family. Please God, in thy great goodness and infinite mercy, look down on Simeon, and bring him your comfort.'

Fenn lifted her head, and looked round. All but the arthritic were on their knees, telling God what to do, a God who doesn't listen, a God who is supposed to know best anyway. Why are we on our knees, Fenn wondered. Does God have an ego problem?

On her right, Dodo had smuggled a peppermint into her mouth. Quite rightly, she had decided church was not the place to offer round sweets.

The Vicar really got into his stride, instructing God to look after the Queen, and give wisdom to those in authority. He knelt, with his head heavy upon his hands, an ambivalent synthesis of grovelling supplication, and high-handed instruction.

You're shouting into an empty barrel, Fenn thought. You hear the sound of your own voice returning, and think it's an answer. Quietly, at twenty-five minutes to twelve, on the day of the feast of the Epiphany, falling conveniently on a Sunday this year, Fenn came to the conclusion that there was no God.

With the minimum of fuss, she got off her knees. She sat slightly forward in the pew, careful not to cramp the person praying behind her. She thought of her cousin's son Ray, lying, unaware of the world, in his hospital bed in Adelaide, and felt a physical pain for him, under her ribs.

'Behold the blessed sacrament of bread and wine,'

said the Vicar, and nodded for the first communicants to walk to the altar.

Hughie watched carefully for the right moment to stand up, it was important not to form an unseemly long queue, but on the other hand, there should be a steady flow. He judged the moment perfectly, and expected Fenn to stand up as well. Instead, she stayed seated. 'I'm not going up,' she said.

'Are you feeling poorly?'

'No. Carry on without me.'

'You must go up,' said Pru. 'It looks odd.'

'No,' said Fenn. She tried to smile reassuringly at Hughie, and Pru, and was sorry that she might spoil their visit to the altar.

She watched Damaris walk away, slightly in awe, but that of course was more to do with the choir, than the sacrament. Doug, in his gleaming leather jacket, keys jangling at the hip, walked by up the aisle, his fingertips together, in order to express the sacred nature of his mission; a little awed himself, as he had no idea whatsoever what was expected of him when he arrived.

Fenn felt detached, quite light-headed, surprised at the ease with which she had cut the thread of belief. She waited, very patient and very still, for the moment when she could escape from this alien place.

By the time Hughie got to the altar, he was convinced Fenn was ill, but being particularly brave. It would be something she'd eaten at Dodo's party. Perhaps he should take her outside, in case she was going to be sick. He didn't have his usual problem of wondering how he should compose his face for walking back. It was easy to look too solemn. In some way, he often thought, one ought to look slightly transformed.

Fenn looked quite resilient, when Hughie got back. He noticed, however, that she failed to make a private prayer before leaving, which always seemed polite. The

Vicar leaned questioningly towards her, as he took her hand at the door. 'We're here as requested, William,' Fenn said briskly, and it sounded more like an end, than a beginning to a new regularity.

Only when they were safely free of the dust and sanctity of the church building did Hughie and Pru attack from either wing.

'Bit of a funny thing to do, wasn't it, Fenn?' said Hughie. 'I mean, you're not ill at all, are you?'

'What will people think?' asked Pru. 'It wasn't as if there were an early service you could already have been to.' Pru pulled on her gloves particularly vigorously. 'They must have thought you'd done something absolutely awful. Committed a mortal sin.'

Fenn dodged ahead, caught Damaris by the hand, whispering to her, 'I've guessed why you're here this morning.'

'Piss off,' said Damaris. Murray must have seen her pass the choir stalls on the way to the altar, he must have felt her look, but he'd never glanced at her once, as the choir left the church.

'You could say,' Fenn called back, 'I've seen the light.'

'Conkers,' said Hughie. 'You won't spoil Sunday lunch, will you?'

Later that evening, at the station, Pru stood by the carriage door and said, 'You can always ring me, if you want to talk about it.' Her coat was firmly buttoned up, not because it was cold, but against the life. How warming it would be, to be able to help with Fenn's problem.

'There's nothing to discuss, if you mean about church.' Fenn looked at her sister, clutching her shoulder bag to her coat, which should have been either two inches shorter, or three inches longer, to look anything like elegant. She clasped Pru's forearms in a surge of compassion. 'Can I ring you, when Damaris has left? I'll be feeling dreadful then.'

'Course you can. But the other. The matter of faith,' said Pru. 'I shall pray that you get your faith back.'

'The point is,' said Fenn patiently, 'getting rid of it wasn't easy.'

Hughie held her arm firmly all the way back to the car, as if she were an invalid. He knew that the less said about the problem, the more likely it was to go away.

## Chapter Six

'Can I get anyone another coffee?' Hughie looked forlornly at Damaris and Marie; Damaris was giggling, Marie sniffing, their outsize rucksacks slumped against the chair legs. 'Sydney' said the labels, threateningly.

Dodo ate two doughnuts, but no-one else could face food.

'Don't accept lifts,' said Fenn. 'Promise.'

'Only from big boys,' said Damaris.

'You'll write as soon as you get there. Just a card,' said Hughie.

'I haven't packed any earrings,' said Marie, as if back from the dead.

'The holes will heal over,' said Damaris, then her face screwed up again, with apprehension. Fenn wanted to hug her, but that would be tactless.

Airports lack soul, being about polystyrene beakers, and hardwearing carpet, and shopping opportunities. They smell of plastic and air freshener. Railway stations, on the other hand, can be all heart, pain reflected in the puddles on the platform, the slamming of doors, the smell of engine grease, the smell of the steam, although it's no longer there. They can be all joy, as the carriages slide into view, the glimpses of faces as they are carried further down the platform, the nostalgia of association with Adlestrop, and Anna

Karenina. Terminal four, on the other hand, is not conducive to emotional outburst.

'Will passengers for flight . . .'

'Listen,' said Hughie. 'It's you.'

'. . . go to the departure lounge.'

Fenn breathed carefully. Damaris would hate her to cry. It was the least she could do for her, be a stoical mother. They held each other, as if it were something they might never do again. 'Remember we love you,' whispered Fenn.

The girls walked unsteadily down the tunnel to the departure lounge, unused to the weight of the rucksacks. Marie turned a tearful face to stare back at Dodo. Damaris squared her shoulders and said, 'Marie. Belt up, or else.'

They disappeared, waving. Damaris nipped back to stick two fingers in the air. Fenn found that wonderfully reassuring. No-one mentioned the A-level retake results. It would have been tactless.

Two weeks later, Fenn wrestled with four pounds of wholemeal pastry at the crumb stage. She looked out over the garden, where the earth was cold and hostile. Winter had a lock on the plant life, as well as on her own soul. She wiped her hands, and picked up the letter, to read again for comfort.

'Having a fab time but you've got to keep your shoes on. Bondi beach is full of used needles. Marie got a stabbing pain in her foot, but fortunately it turned out to be a jellyfish sting.

'Met a great fella called Midge. He's taking a year or two out from his course on the History of Revolution. He's with a mate called Uri (short for Urine?) who Marie has taken against, because of the way he eats. You can hear him in the next room. Midge eats quietly, that's because he's mainly on liquids.'

Fenn longed to unburden her heart, to shift the responsibility of caring. Damaris at home was a constant worry, but Damaris out of reach, would be on an unstoppable slide. The temptation to pray was intense. Her knees itched to be knelt on, and her face cried out to be covered. She wanted to shout, 'Please, please, God, keep Damaris safe. Steer her clear of infected needles on the beach. Protect her at cash points at night in Sydney. Guide her to hostels that are not in red-light areas. Please keep my stupid, darling child safe.'

Hughie refused to let his imagination roam around the lurking dangers of Sydney, and would only say, 'She'll be fine. There's nothing you can do. Got her head screwed on. She'll be fine.'

There were two business lunches this week. Fenn hoped the routine preparations would lend shape to her day. She checked the oval serving dishes on shelves in the cellar, wrapped in cling, to keep off the dust. There was earthenware for casual, white for formal. She inspected the onion marmalade, and herb vinegars, and hoped to feel healed. She felt no different.

She put the letter back on the dresser and got on with bringing the pastry together. Leek and potato quiches. Cheap, ordinary ingredients transformed was the name of the game. If you caramelize your onions, and roast your orange peppers, your cooking reputation gets round the working lunch circuit as being sophisticated, but edible. Above all, not expensive. Business lunches were no longer binge opportunities, but healthy extensions of working lives.

Fenn patted and moulded. She felt the spring of the pastry, its cohesion, its elasticity. It wasn't easy, wholemeal, it usually ended up rigid, or falling apart. Today, it seemed perfect, though she always believed a tranquil mind was needed for good pastry.

The bell rang tentatively. It couldn't be Dodo, who usually played a little tune, wasting no end of electricity.

'Hello, Fenn.' The Vicar stood, slightly bowed, in a posture of submission, tilting his head up to gauge his reception. This was usually either over-rapturous, or resistant. This time, he saw resignation. 'Oh dear.'

'Come in, William.' Fenn wished she'd checked through the spyhole. She'd spotted him coming to the house a week ago, from the bedroom window, and hadn't answered the door.

She tried to sound breezy, leading him into the sitting-room. 'Coffee?'

'I'd really like some water. If I ask for it here, it'll come out of a bottle, and have little bubbles winking at the brim. An extravagance in a clerical home.'

'Ours is extra sinful. It's not English.'

Fenn took as long as she dare, pouring the water in the kitchen, opening a new lemon, and adding ice. She hadn't been looking forward to this inevitable confrontation.

'Well now, I suppose I'd better come to the point,' said William, reluctantly, after a few thoughtful mouthfuls. 'I've been round to see you a couple of times, but you were out. You, er, failed to take the Sacrament at Epiphany, and haven't been in church since. Have I reason to be concerned, I ask myself?'

'You do, and you don't,' said Fenn, poking at her lemon slice with a finger, trying to dislodge a pip.

'You're attending another church? I'd be sorry. Your slightly aloof presence is always welcome, more, I might say, than some of the ardent and more demanding. Oh dear, I shouldn't have said that.' He slapped his hand over his mouth, pretending to have offended, like a child.

'I'm not going to church at all.'

'Aaah. It happens. Yes. Now, then. You've lapsed, would you say? Perhaps lapsed is too strong a word. I mean you've, er . . .'

'Lapsed from what?' Fenn began to feel annoyed. Why should this man feel so certain he had the truth on offer? 'I've decided,' said Fenn, 'there is no Christian God.'

'This is serious. You don't mean it, of course. Remember, my dear, that God loves you, whatever you feel.'

'Even if he doesn't exist?'

'Certainly. No, I mean. Well, yes. There are mysteries which can't be explained, Fenn, and such things have to be taken on faith. Shall we deal with the subject in greater depth when you're feeling a little clearer in your mind?'

'William,' said Fenn gently, 'has it ever entered your head you might be wrong?' She looked down at her hands, and the sun, through the window, caught the red lights in her hair. She wished that, in trying to be honest, she didn't sound so aggressive.

William took another swallow of mineral water, as if to strengthen himself, and made a counter challenge.

'Don't you feel empty?'

'Yes. Obviously. I've answered your question, now. What about mine? Do you ever question your faith?'

'I take care not to. The Bishop has a very strong line on doubting clerics. Too harsh in my opinion, by far.' William swallowed down the last of his water, rather quickly, and stood up, smoothing over the bulges his knees had made in the legs of his trousers. 'Shall I drop some reading matter round? I don't seem to be talking you out of your problem.'

'There isn't a problem.'

The Vicar did not quite manage to unfold his full height, the burden upon him almost visible. 'You can always ring me.'

'Thank you, William.' Fenn clasped his hand in both her own, 'I'm sorry . . . sorry I haven't been entirely satisfactory.'

The pastry was half into the flan rings, tantalizingly in one piece, teasing that it would break into many. The bell went again, strident, and for longer than necessary.

Fenn opened the front door, and Doug strode in. She'd forgotten it was his day. He had his usual smell of joss stick about him, and seemed to be trying to suppress wind in his throat. Mondays were always like this, presumably because of how Doug spent Sundays. Recently, he'd taken to ringing the front doorbell, instead of the back. He carried a large tin of beeswax polish from Jason Antiques. 'The best,' he said. 'Five pounds fifty.'

'Sainsbury's own brand is what I like,' said Fenn, annoyed. 'It's probably exactly the same as that, only you're paying for a fancy tin.'

'Quality, Mrs M. Never underestimate quality. It's quality that shows class.' He threw his bomber jacket over a chair and walked vigorously into the kitchen to find dusters. Fenn noticed the label in the leather jacket, and tried to work out what that had cost. Pity to waste so much money on any jacket that would always look comic over Doug's stretched-to-bursting tartan shirt. She wondered why, also, if he was concerned with class image, he still wore his hair in a ponytail.

Doug sampled the raw pastry on the board, leaving wholemeal flakes on his bright pink lower lip. 'Did I tell you, Mrs Lomax has asked me to take her on? Very nice lady, she is. Told me she was brought up in India. Suits me, as I'm strictly upwardly mobile these days. There's a class revolution, isn't there? Your Royal family are getting real common in parts, I'd say. Know what my ambition is? Open a London branch of Vroom and be taken on by Mrs Thatcher, or Lady Thatcher, as I should say. Have to remember not to call her Maggie to her face. Not unless she asks me to, of course.'

'You'll be sending me one of your employees soon.' It wasn't easy for Fenn not to sound hopeful.

'You were my first, Mrs M, after the job opportunity scheme got me going, so I won't drop you, you'll be pleased to know.' He relished the small shudder which passed across her smooth forehead, like a scurrying wavelet. 'I'll look after Mrs Lomax myself too, she's a real lady. Frail too. Unlike her coming up the path now,' he added appreciatively. May Lomax's distancing of herself, when he had shaken hands after the interview, had not gone unnoticed.

'It's Dodo. Right, Doug. The dining-room first, please.'

Dodo let herself in through the back door. She wore a loose smock in the mistaken belief that it made her look slimmer. She'd abandoned the bohemian image of the party, and gone for Earth Mother mode. She'd given up make-up, and scrubbed her cheeks to a rosy glow. On her feet she wore school sandals. Fenn couldn't imagine where she'd got them. Normally Dodo favoured espadrilles, or boots. She accepted a mug of coffee, and slumped down at the kitchen table.

For a moment, Fenn knew she hoped Dodo was going to talk about Lex, though not that she was getting on well with him. Fenn made some more coffee, Dodo never having only one of anything, and frowned as she fitted a clean filter. She didn't see herself as a bored housewife, who let her mind range over random men.

'Morning,' said Doug, who'd not left the kitchen. 'By the way, we're out of Windolene.'

'Leave the windows then.'

'Good morning,' said Dodo, and automatically lowered her eyelids just a little. 'I hear you're going to help

May Lomax out. She could do with it. She's going round the twist, you know. Left a note on the door for the baker, yesterday, asking him to leave three tea cakes. We haven't had a baker's round for twenty years.'

Doug looked at Dodo, noting the amply filled smock. He liked a rounded woman. A Rubens man himself. He greatly admired Rubens because of his lack of interest in clothes. He'd become acquainted with the artist's work, having been given a classy box of chocolates by a client the Christmas before last. The Allegory on the Blessings of Peace had decorated the lid. Rubens certainly knew how to paint boobs.

'You might be after my services yourself, per-haps?' Doug was surprised at Dodo's civility, and felt he could afford the innuendo. 'With Mrs Lomax and Mrs Meadowcroft both on my books now, we can't have you left out. I was saying to Murray, my son, I'd like the whole of Springfield Lane as my patch.'

'Murray?' said Dodo, thinking she would have ex-pected Doug's son to be called after an American cowboy filmstar.

'Nice name, isn't it? Very suitable for Oxford. I only christened him that last year, when I reassessed my potential. He used to be Robin. It didn't reflect well on me, not after he got into long trousers. I've always said you can't hold a good man back. No such thing as disadvantage. Mrs Thatcher always believed that you know, when she was at her peak.'

Doug progressed to the dining-room with the hoover, and could be heard cheerfully knocking paint off the skirting boards. He sang 'If I had a hammer' with some optimism. Dodo had not visibly recoiled on seeing him, and seemed very impressed with Murray's name.

'He's married, then, the cleaning expert?' said Dodo, ever on the look out.

'Not any more. His wife saw the light some time ago. He lives with his mother. She smokes illicit substances.'

'At least he's a provider,' said Dodo wistfully. 'Heard from Damaris yet?'

'Just a short letter.' Fenn hoped Dodo wouldn't want to read it. No need for her to worry about infected needles as well.

'I've got a short one too. Didn't say much at all. I miss the kid, would you believe? Never thought I'd miss Marie pussyfooting round the flat, doing her good works, and making me feel guilty. I went into her room yesterday, and sat there for about ten minutes, just to imagine her better.'

'I know,' said Fenn. 'I can't get on with things.'

'They're easier to love when they're not under your nose.'

Fenn nodded. 'You forget the faults.'

However, Dodo was unsuited to mother mode for long. She took a noisy slurp of coffee, and said, 'Do you think Lex is too young for me?'

'Too young in what way?'

'As a lover, of course.'

'Is that what he is?' Fenn got up from the table, and went back to her flans. She needed to occupy her hands for some reason.

'Not yet. But I'm working on it. Of course it would only be a temporary arrangement. Until I find a good provider. It's not that I'm mercenary. You know that. But at my age . . . Would you say he's too young?'

'You're a free agent.' Fenn sliced the leeks, while the pastry rested, and then felt able to look at Dodo. She might be over-weight, but her full cheeks were dimpled, and her skin downy, like a plump nectarine. Dodo was not unattractive. 'Lex isn't that young,' she said. 'Older than he thinks he is.'

'I don't know what to do next. What would you do?'

70

'I'm not in that situation.'

Dodo narrowed her eyes, not seductively, but in speculation. 'It might not be out of the question.'

'What do you mean?' Fenn tried to cut the white part of the leeks as thin as paper.

'Lex talked to you a lot at my party.'

Fenn shrugged her shoulders. 'He had to talk to someone. You were busy.'

'Mean and moody. If he looked more practical, I could get him to put up a shelf. What do you think?'

'I think it's you who's losing your marbles, not May.' Fenn hacked at the tougher green sheath of the last leek, and the knife slipped. Slowly, some blood crept out of her thumb. 'Now look what you've made me do.'

'Not like you to be so clumsy,' said Dodo, and the speculative look changed to a small frown.

# Chapter Seven

'We should cheer ourselves up,' Dodo said when she saw Fenn in Waitrose. Her life was a structure of little treats to cheer herself up. 'Let's go to the Mellowstones viewing day.'

'We could take May,' said Fenn. 'The house is already sold as a retirement home. It might be a tactful introduction.'

'This afternoon, then.'

Mellowstones was the Big House when Springfield Lane was a village. Now, built all around, and part of the outskirts of the town, it was difficult to imagine how well it once stood, when surrounded by pasture land. Early Victorian, it was built to show the depth of its creator's purse; quality was its hallmark, proportion its measure.

May led them briskly along the road, looking forward to glimpsing a lost lifestyle, some memento that chimed with her own past, a confirmation of her lost years.

Fenn wished Dodo wasn't wearing her purple poncho over banana ski pants. Luckily the poncho was long enough to cover the essential quality of the ski pants, namely the snug fit round the crotch.

It was warm and damply spring-like, in the way that it can be only in February in England, when the snow is at its best over the rest of northern Europe.

She was relaxed in her olive cords and sweater; there was no need for a coat. Her hair swung loose from a shoelace tie. She caught May up, and hugged her arm.

Few people go to previews of old house sale contents with a view to buying. They're there for the day out, voyeurs into finished lives, sniffers up of the past and the forgotten, lusting after the scent of yesterday. Gone now from the Victorian ochre brick house was Mr Chalmers, where he'd lived with an entourage of decrepit servants guarding his frailty and incontinence with increasing inadequacy. His children had put everything into the hands of the estate agent. The house itself was already sold. The new occupants were ready, waiting to be moved *en masse* from a smaller and less adequate retirement home, just as soon as the renovations were complete.

'Funny smell,' said Dodo, as they looked round the hall. 'Umbrellas and galoshes and dog leads.'

The walls, dun coloured, stretched high above the black and white tiled floor, now dusty with dried mud. Some of the large pictures had already gone, sold to new owners importing Victorian class into their own smaller, but tasteful, homes, leaving pale windows of unsmoked paper at intervals up the stairs.

'When this house was at its height, we had an Empire. You'll never know how wonderful India was then,' said May.

'Don't get on to that, dear,' said Dodo. 'We'll start at the top. Servants' quarters.'

After the solid stairs with the mahogany rail and turned wood, there was a second narrow stairway off a passage, with steep treads covered in linoleum, brown, which had turned elephant-coloured through time.

'Can you manage more stairs, May?'

'Of course. I'm quite spry, you know.'

At the top were not only the maids' bedrooms, but the day and night nurseries, children in those days existing publicly only around tea time.

'A rocking horse,' squeaked Dodo, and unwisely, mounted it. 'Tally ho.' She swayed vigorously backwards and forwards, to get some rhythm going. Unfortunately, one rocker was not securely attached, the horse lurched sideways, sending both it and Dodo staggering, crablike, across the room.

It took five minutes to balance the horse on its rockers again, so that it didn't look broken. 'The child in me,' she explained, and began to rifle through a games cupboard. She sniffed at the teddy bears. 'Musty. I bet they've got lice.'

Fenn left her to it and moved onto the night nursery, large and airy, looking out over the long back garden. Through the window, Fenn saw below, walking along the path from the greenhouses, a figure that, to her surprise, evoked a tiny surge of pleasure, created a small need to smile. It wore an enveloping black greatcoat. She couldn't explain why she didn't call out to Dodo that Lex was here.

When they'd admired the black iron fireplaces, and marvelled at the servants bringing coal all the way up here, when they'd explored the assorted cupboards, and found the skeleton of a frog, Fenn and Dodo went down to look at the main bedrooms.

May lingered in the night nursery, leaning on the windowsill. It was a comforting room. She tried to smell the baby powder, and the warm milk again, to catch her own past moments as well as those of the room. She imagined little Rose crying in the night, and being able to comfort her, to feel the warmth of her body through her nightdress.

But the garden below was in daylight, it was not night at all, of course. Across the lawn, among the apple trees she saw Lewis. She would know that walk anywhere.

Quickly, she turned and went out of the room. She must guard against this weakness, this stupid daydreaming, imagining she could see Rose and Lewis again, when they were both gone for good. If she gave in to these needs, she'd be finished.

The rooms on the first floor were large and numerous. 'Someone's going to spend a bomb,' said Dodo, 'splitting them into more smaller ones. *En suite* showers. No baths, the inmates won't be able to get in. Hotel quality carpets, almost certainly crimson and royal blue. Have to be pee resistant.'

As May came down to join them, she coincided with a band of elderly people, directed by a younger woman, and was swept, with them, into a bedroom with peppermint green walls.

'This way. No Doris, please don't sit down on that bed. You know how you seize up.'

'I hope, Matron, that you will see that I have the master bedroom.' This second woman had mauve hair in which one pipe cleaner, acting as a curler, still nestled. 'First call you know, on length of residence.'

'Stay calm, Molly. Nothing is being decided today. This is merely an introduction. Duncan, that door does not lead into the bathroom. It's a wardrobe. Fix your zip.'

May pushed her way out of the room and went downstairs. She went into the drawing room and sat down on a sofa, gripping her handbag, and trying to seem tranquil. With her feet together, and elbows tucked into her sides, she concentrated on breathing slowly. She shuddered at the memory of the proximity of the creaking Doris, and at the discord vibrating from the woman with mauve hair. There must be no more dreaming of Rose, no more Lewis, or she would end up with these people. With Doris, Molly and Duncan. Or worse. What about those not strong enough to make the outing?

'Sorry Madam. No sitting on the exhibits,' said the man from the estate agent.

'What's a sofa for, if not to sit on?' said May.

'It's for selling. You're not at home now, you know.'

'I want to look at the conservatory, there might be some interesting plants,' said Fenn.

'Can't cope with a plant,' said Dodo. 'Even spider plants get suicidal on me. I'm off to the kitchen. I fancy a bit of copper. See you later.' Dodo bounced down the corridor, disappearing into the back of the house like a jolly, but purposeful beach ball.

Fenn walked among the sleeping pelargoniums, the dusty, leathery green leaves, pipes now cold, the earth sour with green moss. This was a house that seemed about to die. Part of it would. Yet it was about to be reborn as something else. This house would be reincarnated. Fenn wondered which life it would prefer. Perhaps it didn't matter. The new life would contain echoes of the old, just as her own house did. Change does not mean reversal, but a realignment. Old sorrows and joys would meld with the new. Nothing was totally lost.

Something touched her shoulder, so lightly that she didn't immediately react. She looked round.

'I wonder if you would help me?' said Lex.

He laughed at her surprise. 'I'm after a fern,' he said. 'Something with character. For the flat. I can't make up my mind.' He leaned against a wicker table, and shrugged his shoulders, letting go of the responsibility. Under his coat his shirt and tie looked crumpled at the neck, as if he didn't care very much for the formality.

It was somewhat at odds with his face, which didn't fit even such untidy observance.

'Everything here looks pretty dead.'

'It's in one of the greenhouses. Will you advise me? It'll mean coming to the greenhouse. We might even be alone. Would that overwhelm you totally?' He folded his arms, and stared evenly at her, inscrutable as a cat.

She found it disconcerting, his half smile.

'It wouldn't whelm me one way or another,' said Fenn briskly. 'It so happens that I'm looking for a plant myself.' She led the way out of the conservatory, into the garden.

'By the way, I finished my book. Almost.' Lex walked behind her down a narrow path.

'What book's that?'

'Philosophy. For use in class.'

'Sounds impressive.'

'It should be mega. I thought I'd told you about it. I liked talking to you.'

Fenn strode on, trying not to smile. Any encouragement would be a mistake. Lex followed, admiring the bounce of her hair as it tugged at the shoelace, in the breeze.

The greenhouses were better cared for than the house. One of the retainers had been younger, though simple, and had been happy to lose himself all day among the plants, more real to him than people. There were geranium cuttings taken in the autumn, in neat rows of small pots, there were Christmas cacti, some of the less exotic orchids, and the strappy leaves of clivia, as well as the ferns.

Lex wavered between a monstrous multi-fronded specimen, with spores on the undersides as big as ladybirds, and something altogether more modest in size. This was a delicate creature, whose stems made an elegant tracery against the glass of the greenhouse, which was lime-tinged with mildew, but translucent in the watery winter sunlight.

'This one,' said Fenn. 'It's uncommon, and it's graceful.'

'You don't think it a bit feminine, do you? Mightn't the big fern make more of a macho statement?' He stood beside it, and arranged his face in a series of pompous expressions, as for a Victorian posed photograph. 'I need a woman sitting beside me,' he said.

'That fern would suffocate you at night. Breathe in more oxygen than you do.'

'Whatever you say. Have to see if it's popular at the auction.'

'Come to think about it, I don't know why I'm looking for a plant. I shan't be able to get to the sale. I'm doing a lunch that day.'

'I'll buy it for you, and bring it round. You can invite me in for tea. Or whatever.' He spoke as if he were not concentrating, leaning over to take a closer look at the plant. Fenn could see, in profile, the fullness of his upper lip, which made him look both sensuous and sensitive. His skin was coarse, grainy, and the lines around the mouth and nose were entrenched.

'There are none I really like. Thank you.' Abruptly, Fenn walked out of the greenhouse. She wanted to get back to the house, but Lex was walking behind her, deliberately slowly, as if held down by his greatcoat. It seemed rude to move away, so they both strolled, as if in no hurry, until the path opened out into the main garden. There was a garden seat at the edge of the lawn, sturdy with hungry, sun-bleached slats. Lex sat down and looked up at Fenn, challenging her to join him.

'Just for a moment,' she said, for the sake of good manners. She braced herself to be pleasant, but firm, if Lex said anything else silly. But he didn't. He sat silent beside her for a while, leaning back on the seat, legs stretched across the path, large feet sticking up in the air. Fenn began to feel comfortable again, and sat back too. The February sun filtered down on them, warm, as if they were old friends.

Around their feet the aconites glinted like Spanish doubloons, gold against the wet dark earth. Fenn could smell the sleeping grass, and everything around was alive. Under the soil was life unseen, the stirring of herbaceous proliferation, and the lushness that would come as the earth continued its ever-renewing and satisfying cycle, rebirth and hope, refreshment and optimism. She leaned down to a patch of iris roots. She peeled off the slimy leaves, exposing the shaggy fan, cut back in the autumn, over the woody and contorted old stock. From the old brown tubers, new pale green leaves pierced, like daggers, through the tired foliage. The smell of the earth, as she touched it with her fingers, calmed her. She felt alive.

In the distance Molly, Duncan and company were tottering over to look at the outhouses. Doris had sat down on an urn of wallflowers, and was being prised off it, by Matron.

Lex stared at them, and grunted. 'What's it all for? Whatever you do, you end up old.'

Fenn thought of May, growing old, returning to her babyhood. She would become incontinent, unable to feed herself. She would sink back again into the earth, which had nurtured her. Even old age had its pattern. May would grow tired. She would be ready.

'I've had a lousy day.' Lex sat up, and turned to face her. 'A sodding awful day. I'm shattered.' He stared hopefully at her, looking for comfort. This time he wasn't taunting her, teasing, mocking, but looking to her for some response. Why did he have to change moods so abruptly, she wondered.

Fenn, full of the optimism the touch of the earth had given her, rashly put her hand on his arm. 'Things change,' she said. 'Spring might come tomorrow.'

Lex put his hand over hers, pinning it down.

Fenn pulled her hand away. 'Sorry,' she said. 'I'm just feeling optimistic for everyone.'

'There you are,' called Dodo, from the terrace. 'No good will come of sitting on a bench with that man, I can tell you.' She had collected May, and had her firmly by the arm.

'That damned woman,' said Lex, under his breath, and sank down further on the bench.

'Why aren't you teaching?' asked Fenn, sitting very neatly now, while Dodo and May strolled across the grass.

'Don't ask me,' said Lex.

'Where are you, exactly?'

'An out-of-date backwater called St Anthony's.' He raised an eyebrow, and looked sideways at her.

'Hughie didn't say.'

When Hughie's father had bought this house, it became the Old Vicarage, the new and real Vicarage being '46 vintage, flavourless and bland, incongruously nearer to the church. The calling stayed with the old house, there still lurked an aura of imposed goodness, and unquestionability.

In the bedrooms only had Fenn banished the past. Damaris had chosen to surround herself with black and ivory. Elsewhere were clear aqua, soft limes and buttermilk, so the rooms seemed full of light and hope. But downstairs, Hughie had grown tremulous at any suggestion of change to the dark green walls of the sitting-room, or the William Morris flowers in the hall.

That reproductions of the original design were always available was proof to him of their timeless value. Over the years Fenn had slowly introduced some brilliant white paint which showed off the dark colours more effectively. Gradually, she'd moulded the house into a fresh entity, while losing none of the *gravitas* of the years that had slipped away. Now, they lived with the unchanging values of William Morris, in considerable comfort. Fenn was well aware it was family money that kept them this way.

The nadir of her husband's taste, or zenith, if you happened to be Hughie, was the study, the only room where Fenn had no influence. Here the brown paint was intact, the walls covered in books no longer read, but once loved by his father, and even grandfather, their genuine dust hinting of ages gone, of ideas now forgotten. Here, were dark velvet curtains, and lamps whose light-casting ability was seriously curtailed by the abundance of floral representation on their shades.

It was a paradox, she knew, that she didn't love the brown room more. It was in Hughie's certainty of knowledge, which hung on him like a second tweed jacket, she'd recognized her own destiny, and fallen in love, without thinking.

By the time Hughie came home, the kettle was about to boil. She knew immediately, by the way he walked, there was something on his mind. 'Sit yourself down. I'll be along directly,' she called. Hughie picked the cat from his favourite deep chair and laid her out on his knee. Books keep you sane, and so does a cat. Particularly Mysterium, initially named Vodka, being a Russian Blue. This was no problem to her, as she knew herself by other terms quite outside language. It soothed Hughie to talk to her, to look into her deeply uncaring eyes, her unknowable yellow-green eyes with splinters of topaz and ginger lights. 'No wonder the Egyptians worshipped you,' he said, 'Bastet, the cat goddess of the lower fertile Delta.' A cat gives unarguable proof of an intangible soul, and of an alternative plane of life. 'Mysterium, you're so spiritual,' he whispered. 'I have no words for what you are, and it is fitting that, being a cat, neither have you.'

After considering Mysterium's spiritual tranquillity, Hughie felt better, or would have done if he'd not also felt mildly guilty. There's no place in the Christian teaching for the animal soul, even though the occasional oddball Vicar did give a pets' service to lure in the young, and the unhinged.

This afternoon especially, he needed Mysterium's soothing council. He'd had a frightful day. He couldn't get into the staff's stupid heads that Shakespeare didn't need to know about deconstruction to write *Hamlet*. Or that *Great Expectations* would have been no better if Dickens had been a modernist. If only he could get on with the important task of showing the joy of books, instead of treating them like cryptic puzzles. Literature is the shortest distance between two minds, he'd always believed, and neither the theories of Derrida, nor Lacan, would ever convince him otherwise.

Fenn poured tea into the cup, and made the spoonful of sugar ever more meagre. Soon she'd have Hughie off sugar altogether. It was her favourite time of the day, when Hughie came home from school promptly, and they'd have a civilized cup of tea, with sometimes a slice of toast, or a sandwich, before he got on with his marking. He seemed to enjoy the tranquillity of the ritual. 'Not many people have afternoon tea now,' he often said.

But this afternoon he wasn't smiling, nor savouring that first hot gulp. He looked agitated. He sat forward instead of sinking back in the chair. Mysterium had offloaded herself from his knee in a huffy leap.

'Yes?' asked Fenn.

'I shouldn't get annoyed,' said Hughie. 'It's nothing. Not my business.'

'You'll tell me in the end, so why not now?' Fenn smiled at him, but wished this request for comfort had been less as to a mother, more explicit, more like that of Lex.

'Temporary staff. They're never any good, you know. Don't fit in with St Anthony's. I like to think we do things differently there.'

'Is this one worse than usual?'

'They're increasingly worse than usual. Added problem is that I know him. It somehow makes me more responsible for him. It's that bloke who lives in Dodo's top flat. Do you remember him? Lex. What a name. I ask you.'

Fenn said, trying to sound surprised, 'I imagine Lex would be difficult to fit into St Anthony's.'

'His qualifications seemed excellent. Wide experience. A bit too much, perhaps. He seems to have worked in an awful lot of schools. But he won't stick to the syllabus. Now there was double English this morning and he should have been half way through *Henry IV*, part one. Do you know what he did? Put an episode of *EastEnders* on for half an hour. *EastEnders* wasn't even on that ridiculous list of television English that came out. Then he asked them to compare the two. Can you imagine? Comparing the flower of English literature with some droppings from the gutter.'

'One episode of *EastEnders* was called Chekovian in the *Independent*. I expect he's only trying to get children to relate to Shakespeare.'

'Link Shakespeare with what's written for the unwashed masses? Fenn, I wouldn't have expected you to say that.'

Fenn poured Hughie a second cup of tea, and was

more lavish with the sugar this time. She decided it would be tactless while Hughie was so upset to point out that Shakespeare wrote for the masses as well as the Royal Court, and even Royalty didn't wash very often in those days.

'Another thing. Started what he calls a philosophy debating club in the lunchbreak. I mean philosophy, that's university stuff. Way above the heads of even our best. Thursdays is extra Rugby coaching in the lunchbreak. Potter gives up all his time to it. They need that coaching. The first fifteen haven't won a single match this term. Short of creative refereeing by Potter I don't see they ever will. But now half of them choose to go to this philosophy caper because it's indoors, and they can give themselves haemorrhoids by sitting around on the radiators. And do you know what this . . . this philosophy turned out to be? A discussion on proportional representation. Is the man a Liberal Democrat or something? Doesn't he know we have the finest democracy in the world, the pattern for every nation emerging out of the jungle? It's asking for trouble, I'd say. Suppose the wrong side won? You can't be sure these open discussions won't get out of control. Children don't need to discuss things. They need to be told. By people who know.'

'Oh dear,' said Fenn, 'I wonder what he'll be on by the end of the term.' She walked over to the window, and wished she could feel more supportive and loyal about Hughie's pedantic and pedestrian teaching methods. Lex must seem like a breath of fresh air in the school.

'I very much hope he won't be here by the end of the term. Surely poor Woodhouse will be off sedation by then.'

Lex stirred his cuppa soup, and drank half in one continuous gulp, wondering what flavour it was meant

84

to be. He couldn't be bothered to look at the packet in the wastebin. If he knew, it probably wouldn't make any difference to the taste. He caught sight of the coffee spots on his shoes. He wondered if Fenn had noticed them. Probably.

Today had been lousy, although it had started well. There was a letter from Granpy, always a pleasure, though an infrequent one. He was teaching himself Russian, but was inclined to mix up the Cyrillic and Greek alphabets. He'd had a poem published in the local newspaper. Would Lex consider a walking holiday with him in the Cheviots?

Granpy had always been more of a friend than a relation, ever since Lex was a child. For one thing, he was fiercely independent, refusing the protection of the family when Grandmother died. He was never an uninvited presence. For another, he loved to impart knowledge, books, history, places he'd visited. He brought them alive, he was a lamp in the dark. But he never talked about himself, that was his charm, he found everyone else far more interesting. It was through his influence that Lex became a teacher.

Lex chuckled, and felt strong enough to get on with his work before breakfast. He sat at the keyboard and finished the final chapter, twenty by number. It was done. Finished. But not yet a book, not until it was born into print. There it would nestle, his child Idea, in a cradle of hard cover, sheets of white, beamed upon by the midwife publisher. The book was yet but conceived, a union of man and word, and must stay in the womb of this room until a publisher was found. There was always the possibility that it might abort.

Lex risked being late for school to write a covering letter, so he could post it at lunchtime. This, he didn't do, in the event, because he forgot it was the philosophy club on a Thursday.

The club was coming on well, increased from just three children not as clever as they supposed, to fourteen, which was a substantial part of the rugby fifteen, and who were more intelligent than anyone had yet discovered. Most satisfying was that they only arrived at first to get away from Potter's sadistic training, and make fun, but got drawn into the game of discussion.

The group, today, was going well on proportional representation when Potter burst in and caused such a scene.

Reynolds was in fine voice on the dangers of an elected dictatorship, the gist of which he'd lifted from Matron's copy of the *Mirror*, when Potter flung open the door so vigorously that it bounced back off the wall, almost spewing Potter back out into the corridor. The games' master was further put out to hear Reynolds saying with accurate mimicry of the long vowels and deliberate lowered tone, his school bag hung over his wrist like a handbag, 'One does not . . . I repeat . . . does not, allow that sort of thing to happen, in Great Britain today.'

'Philosophy,' snorted Potter, 'seems to require sitting on desks, not at them. This school is meant to be the last bastion of civilization, not some club for Greek pansies.'

'Sir,' said Reynolds. 'There's none of that here.'

'The philosophers were though, weren't they? Plato, Socrates, all buggers the lot of them.' Potter had been plucked, in the best private school tradition, from the army, and very good he was at his job, if that job were knocking unacceptable yearnings out of boys on the sports field. If, on the other, it was to instil a love of games, then he was not.

'I'm three short of a scrum, and I want that put right this minute. Permanent staff have first call over temporary, you'll agree. You two, and you as well. Out. Thank you, Mr Philosopher, sir.'

'Should we debate if Mr Potter behaved well?' suggested Smith.

'Got a better subject for next week.' Lex wasn't certain he dare let them loose on 'Morality without a god'. He'd be slung out on his ear for Jesus bashing. At St Anthony's, atheists remained in the closet. Altogether, it hadn't been a good morning.

Lex went into the next course of his supper which was a Swiss roll. He first opened it last week, and it was now stale. He reread the letter to the editor and decided to rewrite that, give it a bit more panache.

He felt enervated. Potter's fault. Well, partly Potter. It was also Head of English who'd got at him, Meadowcroft. You could see telling people off got him in a state. He hated doing it. It wasn't so much that he was on Potter's side, because he clearly felt no warmth towards Potter, so he'd got onto the 4b's English, and told him not to put *EastEnders* on the video ever again.

'I think everyone should,' Lex said. 'It worked a treat.' But Meadowcroft wouldn't listen. The class discovered Shakespeare had a broader canvas, and was better at quotations. Meadowcroft should rejoice.

But he wouldn't be rejoicing, would he? He'd be moaning to his wife about Lex. The enigmatic Fenn, with crazy hair, and a face pale as the moon, would be comforting Hughie, probably at this very moment. Trying to cheer him up with that smile which seemed to bubble up from within, when she should be comforting Lex.

## *Chapter Eight*

Dodo wasn't a dirty woman; she bathed or showered every day. But she wasn't averse to dust, or grease on the stove, or splashes on the table. Contemplating all of these now, on an empty spring Saturday morning, she wondered if she should employ the services of Doug. If May and Fenn allowed him over the threshold, then surely she could. The sun, filtering through the high window, permanently clouded by saucepan vapours, was, nevertheless, strong enough to highlight the dull film on the doors of the units, the limescale around the taps. Getting up to her elbows in detergent, or chipping away with a fish knife at the grey deposits in the sink, seemed to Dodo, not to be the work of one seeking a fulfilled sensual existence.

Why she hadn't yet contacted Doug was partly the money, and partly the way he looked at her. You might call it natural lust, and Dodo was something of a snob when it came to middle-aged men with ponytails. It was the same thing as a bald-headed man driving a sports car, only more naff. Of course, Dodo was not against age itself in a man, for it often signified money.

When the doorbell rang, she saw through the spy that it was Doug himself. She felt a thrill of pleasure, not because of his attractions, or even his usefulness, but because of the coincidence. That she should have been thinking about him, and immediately he was at the door, was a coincidence. On the whole, coincidences were lucky. They were, Dodo believed, where the paths of fate cross. Coincidences were evidence of the reality of the fates which guided one's life, and therefore gave it structure and reassurance. Dodo believed in God, of course, but he was male, and therefore not totally reliable. There were better indicators that one was cared for; horoscopes, biorhythms, and getting patience out three times in a row. They were rather like God's computer for regulating our lives. Hard evidence of their existence was more comforting to Dodo than the operator, who was usually out to lunch, when she called.

'Yes?' said Dodo, disguising her pleasure, in case it was misconstrued.

'Can I come in?' Doug seemed to lurk on the flat landing, glancing cautiously down the stairs to May's door.

'No.'

'I like a woman that knows her mind. I don't want to talk on the stairs. It's about Mrs Lomax.'

'Yes?'

'Is she all right financially? She keeps forgetting to pay me. Never went to the bank. That sort of thing. I don't think a lady forgets about other people's money. Lucky, of course, that I can afford not to keep pressing her.' He beamed, smug, and shiny about the forehead.

'Mrs Lomax has no financial difficulties. Going a bit soft in the noddle, poor May. We have a civilized arrangement with the rent. Bankers order.'

There was a thump on the stairs from the top flat, as Lex came down them, two at a time. He looked as if he hadn't yet washed his face, as if he might still smell of sleep, but he was whistling. He'd had his hair cut.

Now that it was shorter, his face looked craggier, more rugged. He wore a red T-shirt, which, it crossed Dodo's mind, he might have slept in.

'Lex,' said Dodo. 'Would you . . .'

'Cheers,' he said, 'the post's come,' and disappeared down the stairs. Dodo recomposed her face, so that Doug wouldn't see her disappointment. Lex seemed to want nothing to do with her, ever since he sat on a bench at Mellowstones, talking to Fenn. That was several weeks ago.

'So you think it OK about Mrs L, then?'

'Of course.'

'I was wondering, also,' said Doug, actually wondering if the ample sample was softening up a bit, 'if you'd fancy a pub lunch? Just feel like a run in the country myself, and a bit of intelligent company.' Ploy number one, always tell an ugly woman she's sexy, and a sexy woman she's intelligent. It hadn't been Doug's experience, that either pair of qualities could co-exist.

The whistling returned, and Lex came up the stairs two at a time, carrying his post.

'Thank you,' said Dodo, timing her reply precisely to when Lex was passing. 'Yes, I'd love to have lunch.' After all, Lex was unlikely to know how Doug made his living, and he hadn't even glanced at the ponytail.

Lex was not looking their way, glancing briefly instead, out of the landing window, which gave a view up the road, almost as far as the Meadowcrofts' house.

Doug had given himself a wine education from the helpful comments in the Marks and Spencer wine section. He always felt safe with Marks and Spencer, especially as, like himself, they had gone more upmarket in recent years. So now, as he had a quick shower, just in case, he considered which pub would give the best impression of him. He finally decided it would be wiser to go where he wasn't known at all; he wouldn't need any coarse comments from friends today, with Dodo being a bit of a class bird. He would try somewhere new in the spirit of exploration, and pursuit of good pub food. He would be certain to get in about his Greek holiday. That should impress. He didn't think any of the people he cleaned for went for holidays *sur le continent*.

The date started well. He loaded up the van with his laptop computer, and made a great show of taking it off the front seat, before Dodo heaved herself in. With commendable restraint, he refrained from helping her, that would look like sampling the goods. Passing the shops, they saw May Lomax wandering along. Only Dodo sliding down in the seat prevented him from giving her a tootle on the horn.

They arrived at the Singing Cow in Suttling Parva, which sounded attractive, and looked quaint from the outside. He picked up the portable telephone, then said, 'I think I'll leave this unsociable instrument in the car,' to earn him bonus points for considerate behaviour. Besides, it was out of order, and to carry a telephone, and not actually receive any calls would be counter-productive. By the time they were seated at a small table with uneven legs, immediately behind the door to the kitchens, Doug realized, too late, the Singing Cow was a far from perfect choice.

It lacked reproduction sporting prints, polystyrene beams, brass-coloured fittings, and properly-dressed gentry. The clientele was bovine, earth in their pores, and disdain in their eyes. Snooker was on the television screen above the bar. There were continuous pinging bleeps from the fruit machine. Their laminate table top was smeared, and the smell of wet dishcloth hovered above it.

'Wonderful life in the isles of Greece,' mused Doug, wincing as the kitchen door hit him between the shoulders. 'Lord Byron, the poet, was very fond of Greece you know.'

'Really?' said Dodo, and skilfully shoved the table nearer to Doug, to give herself more room, increasing his vulnerability. She already regretted this lunch, having agreed only to spite Lex, which was pathetic. It had been a tricky moment, when she'd spotted May. May would be a dreadful snob about going out in a van.

'Yes?' said a youth in a tartan shirt, which wasn't tucked in. He looked very like Saturday staff.

'Shall we try the chicken in a basket? Not many places still do it. Very nice chicken they did in a little place I found on Kos.' Chicken always had to be a bit classier than pasta, in Doug's book.

Dodo shook her head, and scowled. She resented the van, the venue, and Doug's appearance. What depressed her most was that she should be making do with so little. The only real comfort, the only one which didn't let you down, was food.

Dodo craned her neck to inspect the menu on the blackboard above the bar. There was no need to impress Doug by ordering a healthy and feminine salad. 'I'll just have chips,' she said. 'And some bread and butter.'

'We don't do bread and butter,' muttered the youth.

'Do you have some bread?' Doug saw his chance to be masterful and ingenious.

'Yep.'

'Any butter.'

'Spec so.'

'Then please bring the lady some chips, some butter and some bread. A little rabbit food to go with it, Dodo?'

'No thanks.'

'I think you'll like the Chablis I've chosen. Peruvian. Very good because of the Spanish influence, you know.' To be fair, this was not one stocked by Marks and Spencer, but it was spectacularly cheap.

'The hotel where I was staying, had a happy hour from seven to eight, but the bar just down the track started half an hour earlier. Got that sussed the first night. So I got an extra half hour in of freebie. Take a tip from me, get your happy hour sorted out, and the holiday will look after itself.'

'All those gods,' mused Dodo, 'Aphrodite and Zeus. Did you see lots of temples?' She felt obliged to try to sound interested. Why hadn't she noticed Doug's spots before? All three were at peak maturity.

'Did a one-day trip. Saw the Asclepi-something, where this doctor from Ancient Greece worked. Hippy whatsit. I'm telling you Dodo, you really get a bit of culture in those places. You could cut it with a knife. They were light years ahead of us then. I expect they were doing heart transplants, while we were still in mud huts.' He paused to allow the food to be put on the table. The chips looked fine, being frozen, and having little contact with the kitchen staff, but the chicken had dried out, with fissures crazing the meat, so that it looked like a baked river bed. The bread was in the form of a king-sized baguette.

'Fascinating,' said Dodo, slicing the bread firmly in half, and spreading it thickly with butter. She then stuffed the baguette with chips, using her pudgy fingers, and licking them, making a sturdy, and bulging chip butty.

Doug was disappointed. He was out with what he'd supposed was a class bird, one he'd have expected to ask for the most expensive mineral water. Instead there she sat, clasping her chip butty in both hands and trying to open her mouth wide enough to get her thick lips round it. His mind played, momentarily, with the symbolism, but Doug was not, on the whole, a man who lived within the imagination.

He ate his chicken without enthusiasm. 'Of course, I

had to leave Mother behind,' he said. 'Fortunately, she survived.'

Dodo closed her eyes and savoured the contrast of hot potato and ice cold butter, the texture of soft bread and crisp chip, hot fat and cold crust. There is nothing in this world like a well-salted chip butty. She took a drink of wine to strengthen her for the next onslaught, and had a brief choke. It was difficult to believe that an innocent grape could ever come to this. The wine tasted like water from a vase, where the flower stems have gone slimy. She remembered when she'd taken a specimen to the antenatal clinic in a gin bottle, and it had been nicked from her basket in the marketplace.

'You can tell it's had a long journey,' she said, mellowing as the carbohydrates hit the system, and brought their comfort.

'My mother's a wonderful woman,' mused Doug. 'Grows her own cannabis.'

'How enterprising,' said Dodo, before she rammed the baguette back into her mouth.

'Bought a vibrator last month, and she's a good seventy-nine.'

Dodo was into her second mouthful. The butter slid down her chin, and onto the front of her blouse.

In other circumstances, reflected Doug, he would have been the first to help mop that up. Disappointment overwhelmed him. He had planned this carefully, he was dining above his station, with possible later options, and here Dodo was, behaving worse than Ma. If he hadn't bought that dreadful wine, he'd be round his second pint of lager by now, feeling jolly as a bishop. 'She says she needs Vaseline now though.' He kept going with the conversation, determined not to let his regrets show.

Dodo looked at him, as she ground down the crusty bread. One of Doug's spots had passed the point of ultimate tension, and exploded. 'Your mother,' said Dodo, the pustule, snake-like, mesmerizing her eyes, 'sounds disgusting.'

'My mother,' snarled Doug, across the table, 'may have spent the odd night in a police cell, but she's a lady. She always paid her fines on the nail. Never kept Her Majesty waiting for money. Not like your snooty Mrs Lomax, who thinks she's too good to be in the same room with me, but never's got the readies on her. Or Fenn Meadowcroft, who thinks she runs the earth. She certainly runs that husband of hers, and he's a bleeding snob, I'd say. Or you, eating like Billy Bunter, and showing me up in a county noshery.'

Dodo carefully selected herself a paper napkin from a pile on the end of the bar, and wrapped up the rest of her chip butty. 'I shall,' she said, 'pay for myself, and be grateful if you'd take me home immediately.'

'De-lighted,' said Doug, feeling more on familiar ground, 'and I'll tell you now, I won't be coming in for coffee.'

# Chapter Nine

May was happy. There were daffodils everywhere today, on the altar, on the pedestal display, and on the windowsills, for it was Easter Sunday. Furthermore, she was going to have lunch with Fenn and Hughie. It would be beef. Fenn was good at Yorkshires, they always had shiny bottoms.

When the Vicar came down the aisle with the choir before him, May was first to her feet. It was her favourite Easter hymn, 'Jesus Christ is Risen Today.' You got twelve Alleluyas. She breathed in the air of the church, made holy by so many prayers. She felt the peace and security locked in by the old stones, and the stained glass, and wondered how anyone could find strength without such comfort. Today, it felt as if little Rose were there, beside her.

One of the nice things about this Vicar was the extra-long pause you got for your own particular prayer, being able, as it were, to catch the ear of God while he was around, having his attention brought to one, by the Vicar.

'Please help poor Fenn,' she prayed, 'to find her faith. Help me to try to talk to her. Dear God, use me as a channel through which faith can pour.' She sometimes wondered if God were going deaf, like the rest of us. Or if he didn't care a great deal for her, that he found her nondescript, a woman of trivial and bloodless sins.

On the walk home, she passed the old house. There was a sign up now. Mellowstones Residential Home. All through the early spring, there'd been builders and decorators, carpet layers and plumbers. Now it was ready to house its inmates. 'Poor prisoners,' said May out loud. 'Poor Molly and Duncan and Doris.'

She put her hand over her mouth, for being so stupid as to talk to herself, and because the inmates had already arrived. There was Duncan, she recognized him, standing inside the railings, clasping them with either hand, like an animal gazing out from its cage. She passed by, looking at him, ready to give a sympathetic smile. There was no opportunity, he stared out, not seeing her, gazing at another horizon, the boundary of a lost land.

May walked on, jolted, dislocated from her garnered tranquillity. Fleetingly, well ahead of her, she saw Lewis walk round the corner. Such arrogant shoulders. But when she turned into Springfield Lane, he was gone, as she knew he would be.

Take a firmer grip, she told herself. Imagining Lewis and little Rose, who'd seemed to be in church this morning, was to take the path to join the likes of Molly and Duncan and Doris. The present, May, the present, she told herself, is what safeguards your future.

In her small kitchen, which unfortunately didn't overlook the garden, still lingered the faint smell of grilled plastic, the result of what happened on Thursday. Very clinging, the smell of the plastic film, in which supermarkets enshroud their lamb chops.

She expected to smell beef. She looked in the fridge. There was a pork chop. She'd been certain in church she was going to have beef. Never mind, she had parsnips, and some red currant jelly.

She had reached the stage of sliding the chop, the fat gleaming and crisp, onto the plate, when the doorbell rang. It was Hughie Meadowcroft. 'We rather hoped you were coming to lunch,' he said.

'Shall we go to church?' Hughie'd said. 'It's nice at Easter.' His acceptance of the institution was so complete and fond that he rarely needed to go at all. For him, 'let sleeping dogs lie', had a biblical ring to it. But Easter and Christmas were different.

'Do you ever listen to a thing I say, Hughie?'

'I thought, perhaps, with it being Easter . . . are you still an atheist?' He spoke in a hushed tone, as of a fatal illness, yet managed to sound scathing.

'Bit more agnostic now. Still working on it.'

'Agnostic? A don't know? You must know.' Hughie shuddered. 'You'll be voting Green, next.'

Fenn hacked at the Brussels sprouts, incongruously making the sign of the cross on the stalk, but said nothing. How could she tell Hughie how frustrating it was that he never changed any of the opinions he'd held for twenty-five years?

'Couldn't you be just a tiny bit prepared to change?' she asked.

Hughie, breathing slowly and carefully, picked up the cat, and took her to sit with him on the garden seat.

'Oh, Mysterium,' he whispered. 'I know what you feel like when people stroke you all up the wrong way.'

Mysterium had stretched, purred, and settled down on his knee to doze in the weak sunlight, the sound of distant birds being the only thing on her mind.

Hughie was still feeling ruffled at lunch time when Fenn opened the door to Dodo. She had a grasp of Lex by the elbow. 'I knew you meant to include him,' she whispered. 'Anyway, I told him you had. He'd only got Weetabix for lunch.'

Hughie stopped pouring sherry, and took a quick slurp from the glass he held. He topped it up slowly, before carrying the tray forward.

'Welcome,' he said to Lex, with the easy warmth that came with his sort of upbringing. Hidden, totally out of sight, were the thoughts he would express later to Fenn.

Lex held Fenn's hand for ages, and looked at her without saying anything, with just a sort of question in his quizzical eyes.

Fenn, disconcerted, went to check the beef in the kitchen. Lex followed. 'I know you didn't invite me,' he said, leaning on the table with his arms folded. 'Are you cross?'

'Of course not.'

'In the absence of any move on your part, I had to take my chance.'

'This is not a chance, Lex. You seem to have some funny idea about that.'

'Perhaps not a chance,' said Lex. 'Just a step on the way. Let me take the plates for you.'

Lunch was late, with May having to be fetched, and Fenn thought the beef might spoil. As it turned out, the mistake was not serving Yorkshire puddings, but instead, clever little *choux* puffs filled with horseradish cream. May stoically faced yet further proof that she was not loved by God. Fenn noticed the disappointment on her face, and decided to have her round for a Toad-in-the-hole lunch during the week. The puffs were too innovative for Hughie on a Sunday. He ignored them totally.

Fenn loved a full table, for the family to be outnumbered by guests. It was the mark of man's difference from animals that a meal should be creatively convivial, not merely an opportunity to trough.

'How was church, May?'

'The Vicar was on form,' said May. 'You'd have enjoyed the sermon,' which was to remind Fenn she was still lapsed. 'Have you heard from Damaris?' she added, thinking she'd been a bit sharp again.

'On some farm in the outback at the moment,' said Fenn vaguely. The last letter was not reassuring.

'Lucky girls. Out there, with all those sex-starved red necks,' said Dodo, through a mouthful of potato.

'These horseradish things are lovely, Fenn.' Lex looked at her with half-closed eyes as he chewed. His whole body seemed to exude pleasure in them, like a cat writhing with enjoyment at being brushed.

'Good,' said Fenn, and wished he'd behave normally. 'By the way, May, I heard from Pru, yesterday. She's doing a course on fossils. A subject not limited to women, I suppose.'

'Poor girl,' said May.

Dodo didn't like the way Lex was watching Fenn. He'd had his opportunities with herself, and never taken them. She turned her attention to Hughie. Hughie, thought Dodo, there's one I could settle for. He may not be exactly sexy, though quite handsome in a conventional way, wears nice tweedy jackets, doesn't get his hair cut often enough. I wonder if I ought to be showing Hughie a little bit of appreciation? Fenn does take him for granted. Look at him now, being so kind and gentle to poor May.

Dodo watched Hughie, and noted the soft, wide mouth. He had a big nose. That could be a good sign in a man, some would say. What he needed was a motherly woman, an ample woman, who could untangle all those inbred inhibitions. Dodo chewed vigorously on a shining roast potato, savouring on her tongue its richness, and wondered whether an opportunity would arise to help Hughie out.

By talking to May, Hughie was able to deflect the sound of Lex away from him. 'I was wondering, May, if you've heard about this place called Mellowstones?'

May extracted the horseradish from the imitation Yorky, and religiously finished her present mouthful. She put down her knife and fork. 'Anyone can forget about lunch,' she said.

'I'm not suggesting you should be in a home now. But a really good retirement home will have a waiting list.'

'A really good retirement home will be jolly expensive,' said May.

'Not necessarily. Would you like me to make enquiries for you? Just something to have in mind for a later date. A much later date, of course.'

'No.' In her insistence, May tapped the table, and knocked over her glass.

'Don't worry about that, or about the home,' said Fenn soothingly, and mopped everything up. 'Leave it, Hughie, dear.'

May remembered her upbringing, straightened her shoulders, smiled at Hughie. 'Thank you. If that's what you think.' She ate the *choux* puff, and wondered if this were God sorting out her future.

'Did I tell you, Hughie,' said Lex, 'that my philosophy group concluded that the Conservative party and Christianity are mutually exclusive?'

'Hughie, I expect May would like to see the garden,' said Fenn, when the coffee was finished. She hadn't orchestrated the meal at all well, there'd been understated friction throughout. 'Perhaps you could help me in the kitchen, Dodo. Would you like to do the Sunday papers?' she said to Lex, thus arranging the next half hour in a practical way.

Unfortunately, Dodo elected to join Hughie and May, and Lex appeared beside her at the kitchen sink.

*     *     *

May dutifully inspected the rows of spinach and the early broad bean plants. Inspecting a garden requires that every corner must be walked. Dodo led Hughie further from the house, demanding that he should explain the science of composting. Once out of sight of the kitchen window, and of May, she leaned faintly towards him. 'Hughie, I've got to tell someone. That dreadful man, Doug. He insulted me.'

'Doug is a walking insult. He can't help it.'

Dodo took a firm grasp of his arm. She leaned her head on his shoulder, and one very soft sob escaped although her eyes remained perfectly dry. She discovered Hughie's jacket felt comfortingly warm, smelling very slightly of sweat. She was conscious, too, that he was embarrassed.

'There, old thing,' murmured Hughie, torn between feeling the gentlemanly thing would be to pat her shoulder, and the intense desire to prise off her claw-like clasp. 'You'd be better off with Fenn. Always good in a crisis. Let's get back to the kitchen.'

May meandered away from the vegetable garden, coming towards them.

'Thank you, Hughie,' Dodo whispered. 'I feel much better, knowing you understand.' She smiled meaningfully at him, and turned to lead May by the arm, to inspect the apple tree.

Hughie followed, wriggling his shoulder to shake off Dodo's heavy perfume which seemed to still hang round him like a wraith.

'I'm certain you would rather read the Sundays, than wash up,' said Fenn, taking the tea towel off him. 'Please.'

'Why are you so nervous?' Lex had that tantalizing half smile again.

'I'm not nervous.'

'It's the electricity. It's there. You can't deny it.'

Fenn grabbed the meat tin, and drubbed it with the pan scourer, splashing water all about her. Lex came and stood behind her, putting a hand either side of her, on the edge of the sink.

'You're standing far too close. You'll get splashed.' She was aware of the smell of his skin, fresh, like wind-blown washing, no hint of aftershave.

'Not a single part of me is touching you. I have very long arms.'

Fenn thrust the meat tin at him, pushing it, dripping, against his sweater, and handed him the tea towel. 'You very kindly insisted on helping,' she said.

'You seem such an honest person. You're not being honest now, are you?'

'Ready for the gravy pan?' she asked.

'Fenn?'

'Here comes Hughie.' Here comes my other child, she thought, another person clinging to her for survival. If only Hughie would make her laugh, if only he would surprise her, excite her. Fenn smiled at her husband, through the window, as he came up the path behind Dodo and Fenn, but he didn't see her. He was heaving his shoulder around in quite a strange way, shaking it, as if to dislodge something. It was difficult to remember if Hughie, even when they first met, had ever created the unrest in her that Lex, standing so close, had done. Which was ridiculous.

## Chapter Ten

Fenn put the phone down. 'Damn,' she said. 'Fancy
leaving it this late.' The kitchen table was piled with
white boxes, casseroles, and baskets of cutlery.

Dodo picked out another chocolate biscuit from the
tin on the dresser and dipped it into her coffee. Some
of the chocolate slid off as it was on the way to her
mouth. She was waiting to go with Fenn, to help serve
at a lunch. She wore her black tube, which she believed
was suitable. It would have been, in a larger size.

'Cancelled,' said Fenn. 'Three hours' notice. I ask
you. The chicken will go in the freezer. I need exactly
that amount next week. So will the mango mousse,
but what can I do with four dozen goats' cheese *mille-
feuilles*?'

'Oxfam?'

'Course not. Yes. The Vicar's soup kitchen. You're a
genius. I'll take them along there tonight. I could stay
and help out.'

Fenn thought of the generosity of the natural world,
the way she'd felt sitting in the garden of Mellowstones.
Life was generous to her, and now was a chance to
pass it on. She'd tried to be benevolent at lunch on
Easter Sunday, but they were all so unreceptive, Hughie
spitting out his *choux* bun, Lex standing too close. The
homeless would be quite different.

'Hughie will have something out of the freezer. I'll get some salad to go with it, from the garden,' said Fenn, and swirled through the back door.

Dodo saw her opportunity. The idea had been in her mind since Easter. She waited until Fenn was safely among the lettuces, before hiding her own purse under a newspaper on the dresser. She rifled through her handbag, like a hamster turning its playwheel, to find her nail file. With this, she extracted the fuse from the microwave plug. Sometimes, she was surprised at her own cleverness.

The Vicar unlocked the garage. He bent down and squinted at the keyhole, before he could get the key in properly. His shoulders were of an older man than his blond hair suggested. He wore jeans and an Arran sweater which had been badly washed too many times. William, clearly, had dressed with care for the occasion.

Fenn wore her tracksuit, the one for winter gardening, and no jewellery, because of temptation to those she would meet. Her hair was freshly washed, as an example, and entwined in a scarf to limit contamination.

'How are Damaris and Marie getting along?' asked the Vicar, turning the full appeal of his caring blue eyes on her.

'Both got a little job. Hospital laundry, actually. Seeing life as you'd expect. They've left the outback, thank goodness. Dodo and I each had a letter last week.'

'A very spiritual girl, Marie. Frankly, I worry about her.' The Vicar set up two trestles and heaved a board across them. He plugged in the soup kettle to a socket at shoulder height and filled it up from the assorted flasks and buckets he'd brought with him. Fenn unpacked her own basket.

'I was surprised when you rang,' he said. 'I was leaving matters spiritual for a while. Often works best.

105

Now you return to the fold, with practical service to Christ.'

'I wouldn't put it like that,' said Fenn. 'I'm using you. I wanted to help people, yes. But I'm left with an excess of food, four dozen starters which aren't suitable for freezing. There was a cancellation.'

'I see.' William stirred the soup with a long-handled ladle. 'Vegetable. Old Mag's favourite.' He stacked the mugs in neat rows. 'I bet you ten pence that Charlie the Rum 'un will be first. In the collection box if I win, of course.' He giggled. 'What exactly is it you've brought?'

'*Mille-feuille* of goat's cheese and spinach.'

'I was wrong. Here comes Sir Terence. You fill the mugs and I'll hand out. They expect certain words of me. I sometimes think they feed on me, though I can never promise them what's not mine to give. Vegetable tonight, Terence. Not much of a summer evening, is it? Get those extra socks from the welfare now. There'll be some about with the better weather coming.'

'Do have a *mille-feuille*,' said Fenn, spooning soup with one hand, and proffering her basket with the other.

'No thanks, lady. No, guv, they accused me of having a sock fetish. I couldn't get no medical certif like you said neither. Them doctors don't want you on their list, if you look like you're going to cost them anything. Still, the Father knoweth we have need of these things. The Lord will provide.'

'Well done, Terence. Luke twelve, verse twenty-two, more or less.'

'If not, there's the Welfare, though you can't rely, really, on either of 'em.'

'Talk to you later, Terence. Hello, Mags. It's your favourite. No Charlie yet?'

'Charlie's been took.'

'Not by the Lord, I hope?'

'House guest of the Queen. Just a misunderstanding. Charlie didn't explain himself very well.'

'Would you like a *mille-feuille*, Mags?' Fenn smiled encouragingly. 'Homemade, of course. Full of essential vitamins.'

There was something in Mags that made her rise to the occasion. 'Ta.' She selected the smallest slice between forefinger and thumb, carefully keeping her little finger held aloft, as she was dining above her station.

In silence, Fenn watched Mag's face descend the scale from politeness to suspicion, to disbelief, to horror, and then miraculously recompose, and ascend through determination, to courage, to a dogged smile, and finally with the last swallow to assume again, the tranquil blank of acceptance of her lot, before drifting away into the night. Mags had learned early that it was her fate to suffer in this life.

They waited until eight o'clock, getting the late-comers. Vegetable soup is like fishes and loaves in its catering flexibility, thought Fenn, a judicious watering down if the multitude was large, seconds all round if there were not too many.

The Vicar packed up his soup urn and cups into refuse sacks as he had no means of washing up. Fenn looked down at her basket, lighter than when she arrived by one only. She leaned against the door of the garage, her arms crossed. Instead of feeling in harmony with the world, she felt she jangled with it. The dirt and the smell of these people were at odds with the savoury creations, wrapped elegantly in a white napkin, nestling smugly against woven willow. She hadn't been generous at all. She'd been crass and insensitive. She'd been Lady Bountiful.

'Are you going to offer me a *mille-feuille*, Fenn?'

'Mags told one of the men it was like eating a cowpat. Of course, goats' cheese is on the pungent side.'

'Piquant, I'd call it. Absolutely delicious. I couldn't take some home for the family, could I? Imogen doesn't have a lot of time to do the fancy stuff.'

'You are a kind man, William. Making me feel better. They certainly were a disaster.'

'Will you come along again? Potted meat sandwiches go down well for a treat, I find.'

'I don't know. My motive's suspect.'

'What's it all about, exactly?'

'Generosity. Passing it on.'

'Love thy neighbour,' smiled William, holding his palms up, as if showing he'd pulled a rabbit from a hat. 'You'll never be far from the path, Fenn.' He thought turning her belief back in the right direction might be a miracle, but it was only a conjuring trick.

'No, it's not that.'

'What's the difference?'

'The reason for doing it, I think.'

'To follow the teaching.'

'That comes down to bagging a place in heaven.'

'I'd never put it like that.'

'I think you should be generous for no reason at all.'

William leaned back against the wall, his shoulders sagging. 'I envy you, in a way, treading your own path. Not everyone can be free, Fenn. Most need certainty. Offer them freedom, and they'd be lost. My church may not be a sound vessel, but at least it's a raft. Like everyone else, I need to cling on.' He smiled at her, a tired, wistful smile. Away from his vestments, and his clerical cloak, he'd lost his authority, lost the touch of certainty.

'I think you understand me, William.'

'Another one that's got away. What now for you?'

'I'll have to think about that.'

'Let me know what you find out. And I wouldn't mind a bit of help here, another time. Especially with the honesty.'

'Thank you for not preaching. I shan't forget this evening.'

Fenn drove home slowly, the smell of cooked goat's cheese still seeping through from the boot.

Hughie was pleased to see Dodo, when she arrived to reclaim her purse. 'Just the person,' he beamed. 'Could you take a look at the microwave. It won't come on. Fenn left me one of my favourites, but it's not finished defrosting.'

Dodo flicked all the switches, resituated the semi-rigid chicken in Reisling on the turntable, snapped the switch on and off, and on again.

'It's bust.'

Hughie hammered on the glass door. 'Turn on, old thing.'

'It's got to be fully defrosted,' said Dodo firmly, 'or it will get your gut. So you're no good with the ordinary oven.'

'Looks like I'll be having scrambled egg. I do hate it when Fenn's not here.'

'Odd how things turn out,' said Dodo, walking casually to the door. 'I've overcatered on my casserole. Do come over and share.'

'I couldn't possibly do that.'

'Why ever not?'

'It wouldn't be . . . er . . . you know . . .'

'You think I'm going to seduce you. What a vain man. Typical of the breed, I suppose. It's pheasant.'

'I don't think that for one minute. Of course not. It's pheasant? Mother used to cook pheasant. Bread sauce and game chips. Red wine gravy.'

'Hen pheasant. You get a lot of meat on a hen bird.'

109

'I can imagine.'

Dodo opened the back door. 'Don't let your scrambled eggs get rubbery.'

'Do you think Fenn would mind? I mean, she wouldn't like to think of me going hungry.'

'On the other hand, do cook them enough. If they're watery they'll be full of salmonella.' Dodo almost closed the door behind her, then opened it again slightly, to give Hughie a little wave.

'Thinking about it,' said Hughie, 'Fenn would want me to have a proper supper.'

The table was already laid for one. A more worldly man than Hughie might have wondered at the starched napkin and the three iris heads floating in a white bowl. Neither did he appreciate that all magazines, chocolate wrappers, postcards and blouses waiting for buttons were stuffed under the sofa.

Within seconds of Hughie walking cautiously into Dodo's kitchen, a second place was laid, and the casserole was on the table. Dodo knew that Fenn's foray into the twilight world of the homeless might be all too brief.

'Would you pour the wine, Hughie?' She took the bottle from behind the radiator. It had cost her two pounds more than usual.

Hughie was disappointed that his helping of pheasant was so small. He noticed there were no pud spoons. At least Dodo kept filling up his glass.

'You know the food's OK if there's not much talking,' said Dodo, putting the food in her mouth as continuously as a metronome. Hughie found himself gearing up his chewing to match her. As she put in the last mouthful, Dodo went on, 'I'm a Capricorn, did you know? Capricorns are late developers. I believe I must be somewhere near my peak.' She smiled at him across the table, slightly flushed with all the rush, but relaxed now, and exuding a glow of well-being. Delicately, delicately for Dodo, that is, she touched the edges of her top lip with the tip of her tongue. She ran her hand through her hair in a gesture of freedom and release.

'Fantastic meal,' said Hughie standing up, still feeling he was rushing on. Dodo seemed to be loosening up in some disturbing way, limbering up for a new activity. 'I didn't know you could produce a meal like that, Dodo. Thank you. I shall go home, and boast to Fenn how well I've eaten.'

'Did you really enjoy it?' asked Dodo, and stood very close to him. So close that although not touching him, he could feel the warmth of her. The warmth carried the musky smell of her scent.

He backed away. 'Yes. Excellent.'

'Then give me a brotherly peck to say thank you.' She was there again, all that warmth and scent, and he noticed that the buttons of her blouse were not done up as high as they might have been.

He backed nearer to the front door, clashing with the telephone table. Dodo advanced. Now her hand touched his arm. Her eyes, very big and positively lustful, seemed to be swallowing him up. Slowly, smoothly, her hand moved down from his arm, to his chest, and then, amazingly, on down still further.

For the shortest possible moment, Hughie recognized that she was offering a step into a new heaven, the world of pleasure without love and commitment, a chance of losing the inhibitions on which he so carefully constructed his life. An experience so different to that given by Fenn, who aroused his passions by the smell of her garden-fresh Victorian nightdress, and the sight of her hair on the pillow.

It was a wafer-thin slice of time, but that didn't mean it wouldn't exist for ever in his consciousness, taunting him, causing regret, and self congratulation, in turn.

111

Hughie pulled himself together, and behaved in the way that an old-fashioned education always hopes for, but rarely achieves. He grabbed Dodo firmly by the upper arms, pinning them safely to her sides, and holding her well away from him, fired a lightning quick kiss on her left cheek, before making a dash for the door.

Out of sight, up Springfield Lane, Hughie had to lean on his garden wall to recover, his mind awash with conflicting feelings. All were shrouded in a fog of terror. He'd narrowly escaped from a tricky situation. Occasional shafts of light penetrated the fog. He'd really behaved rather well. He'd let down neither Fenn nor Dodo. The kiss was totally brotherly, devoid of anything carnal. Yet another little light told him he might actually be a sexy man, something he never seriously considered.

It was thus that Fenn found Hughie, draped over the garden wall, as she drove back from feeding the homeless.

## Chapter Eleven

When, two Saturdays later, Dodo took Fenn to a meditation day project, she still wasn't certain how much Hughie had told Fenn about the carefully prepared impromptu supper. Until today, she'd kept out of the way.

'Meditation will stop us worrying about the girls,' said Dodo. 'It rinses the mind.'

The class was held in a school room, jolly with paintings of French shopping, and railway scenes, and poems framed with pencil illustrations. On one wall hung a diagram of the tree of life. Their instructor was waiting for them, a young woman, with spirals of limp fawn hair, a white shell suit, and pale pink trainers.

It turned out later that Lauren had studied with a yogi in Agra, though not for all of the prescribed two weeks. She'd begun to doubt his much-mentioned vow of celibacy, and his breath smelled like old seventy-eight records, that stale smell, which is the perfume of junk shops. She had, however, topped up her knowledge with a crammer weekend in Birmingham, where the giver of knowledge was not unlike John Major. It was quite a shock initially, until she realized it wasn't him.

As they spread out exercise mats, Dodo asked, casually, 'Did Hughie tell you I did him supper the other evening. He couldn't make the microwave work.'

'Yes. I meant to thank you for rescuing him.'

'I hope he enjoyed it?' Dodo's tone was light, and careless.

'He loves pheasant. He said it was a nice plump bird.'

Dodo sneaked a glance at Fenn, to work out if the words meant something else. Fenn was taking off her trainers, and not looking at all reproachful. She looked, in fact, Dodo noticed, somewhat younger than usual, wearing no make-up. Her skin taut, with a pearl glow, that brief epidermal flowering, that comes between the plush of youth, and the sponge of age. Dodo concluded, correctly, that Hughie had kept quiet about her intentions. She lay down on her mat, relieved.

'Everyone lying flat, please,' said Lauren. 'First, we must become unaware of the body. Allow nothing else in your mind. Fill it only with consciousness of the breath.' Lauren intoned slowly, forcing down the breathing rate. When she was on her set piece, Lauren's vowels went noticeably upmarket, and she emphasized individual words, like Mrs Thatcher used to, when she was in the wrong. It was not conducive to Fenn's complete mastery of banishing body awareness.

Dodo levered herself up, and fetched her anorak, from the chair behind her.

'Are we cold?' enquired Lauren.

'Blood pressure,' whispered Dodo, tiptoeing back, and mimed that she was going to make it into a pillow.

'Are we allowed to lie flat?' Lauren asked, apparently remembering she'd forgotten the required warning about medical conditions. 'Perhaps the lotus position would be better, after all.' It was her experience, that few ladies on a Saturday course could get into a lotus position, and if they did, could do very little in it, once there. There was always a tendency, either towards locking, getting knotted up for the rest of the class, or for suddenly springing apart, limbs shooting out in odd directions. Generally speaking, the lotus position for beginners was trouble.

'I'll be fine with this as a pillow,' said Dodo, shuddering at the thought of getting her heels up near her groin.

From breathing, Lauren moved onto visualization, and told them to imagine themselves lying on a beach of white sand. She played some seagull and wave music from a tape. 'The mind is emptying of all except the sound of the water. You are at peace. The breathing is in time with the water on the shore. It goes slowly in, and then falls back. Gently. So gently. Now the mind is not aware of the body. It is alone. It moves with the waves. Slowly up the shore, and then falls back.'

'We're going to Corfu in August,' said a woman brightly from the back row. Fenn had noticed her earlier, in a flocked-turquoise track suit.

'We're not in Corfu now,' said Lauren soothingly. 'We're breathing slowly in, and letting the breath fall gently back.'

By lunchtime, Fenn felt mellow. Two hours lying down, tightening and relaxing, breathing and giving herself up to the instruction of Lauren's monotonous voice, was peculiarly soothing. She tried to retain the peace during lunch, over a mineral water and salad in a wholemeal roll.

Lauren sat with Dodo and Fenn, and it was then that the stories about the yogi came out.

'What, exactly, did he do?' Dodo stopped chewing to listen.

Lauren giggled. 'Well, it was more the vibes I was getting, really. I could tell. You can, can't you?'

'You could tell what?' insisted Dodo.

Lauren giggled some more, and had a suppressed choke on her tikka chicken pitta pocket.

'Was he wearing only a loin cloth, then?' Dodo put her roll down.

'Of course not. A robe. Lots of it.'

'What made you start meditation?' asked Fenn.

'It was really because I fancied Imran Khan, I suppose. That bloke that plays cricket. I'd paid the deposit on the holiday before I found out he's a Muslim, and Muslims don't meditate. So now, I've got to recoup.'

By three o'clock, Lauren got their minds sufficiently empty of thoughts to take them further. Even Dodo had given up speculating on the non-sacred activities of the yogi.

'We'll empty the mind as before. Using the diaphragm.' It was strange, mused Fenn, that no-one had pointed out to Lauren that the 'g' in diaphragm is not pronounced.

'It is life. The breath comes and it goes. Comes. And goes. You are aware only of your breath. Now your mind is clear. You have left behind all links with your body. Except your breath. Now you're aware you're not alone. You can feel the great force of energy, which is life.

'The energy you were given at birth. That is with you until you die. Until there is no more breath. You feel that the energy is part of a greater energy. Shared by all.

'You are in touch with the unconscious self, which is older than time, which has always existed. You are in touch with the forces of the universe. All is very still. Very kind. It is peaceful.'

There was a gentle snoring from Dodo as she was lulled into sleep, and forsook altogether the forces of the universe, but Fenn didn't hear her, although she herself was not asleep.

Lauren took them through a second visualization, across mountains and streams, to the white temple where they could hear pure silence. Lauren gently

116

kicked Dodo's foot to wake her up, as the bubbly gurgles were making the silence impossible to hear.

Fenn couldn't quite get herself to the white temple, she could get no further than the stream. There, she felt the water washing over her, taking away her ability to shape her skills and efficiency, her need to form Hughie, and Damaris, cleansing her of power. By the stream, her face relaxed, and she felt a sensation flow through her, like a silent breeze.

Later, she couldn't put into words what exactly she did experience. There'd been a force, an intense feeling of life. There was generosity, but there was no self. There were no people at all, in this place which she couldn't see, but momentarily knew. She thought, perhaps, she'd heard its silent song, in a language quite other.

As they walked to the car park, the woman in flocked-turquoise jogged past, the one who had Corfu to look forward to. She said, 'I thought all that stuff about another energy was blasphemous, didn't you?' She got into a Ford Granada.

'I missed that bit,' said Dodo. 'I wonder if I could afford to go to India.'

'I can understand now why Roman Catholics believe the power of the Pope is transmitted, even when the Pope is bad. He's only a vessel,' Fenn said.

'What?' said Dodo, easing herself carefully into the driving seat. 'Amazing how tiring this sort of day can be.'

'I mean, Lauren wasn't wise, was she? She wasn't spiritual either. But she was a vessel. She was a pathway.' Fenn leaned her head back, turned it, and smiled warmly at Dodo.

'What did I miss, for heaven's sake? You didn't levitate, did you?'

'Not very well. I came up against the ceiling.' Fenn didn't even cringe, as Dodo grated into second gear. She was musing that Lauren was a most unlikely priest.

Fenn prepared supper. The chicken was already in the fridge, in a sauce of oranges and tarragon. She finished the green salad, put it in a clay bowl, and moved on to peeling the potatoes. Softly, she hummed to herself the theme of the Largo in Vivaldi's *Winter Concerto*, its yearning echoing her own reaching out. Glimpses of the same yearning notes were there in the *Summer Concerto* too, sadness in the heat. Why were these notes, each in a minor key, so full of pain, hidden in joy?

Through the window she saw Hughie stab at the rampant red poppies with a hoe. They came every year, at the beginning of summer, brazen and boisterous, not quite in keeping with the rest of the border. Hughie always tried to dig them out in the autumn, but never succeeded. They'd come again, more vigorous than ever. Once there, it seemed wrong to cut them down, not to have their colour.

She felt mellow, she wanted mellowness to flow through her, to infect Hughie. Mellow, and at the same time, vital. The experience she had, so unexpectedly, when all she sought was stress management, a way of keeping her mind off Damaris let loose in the Antipodes, was still with her. She tried to define what she felt, thinking of pagan belief, and of Buddhism, of negative and positive forces forming an equilibrium, balancing and healing. But it was like music, impossible to define through the medium of words. It filled her with vitality.

'I think,' said Fenn, as Hughie walked through the door, 'we should spring clean the study. What about some pretty new curtains.' She felt strong, that it was time to start bringing life up to the mark.

'I like it as it is. Anyway, spring's almost finished. Too late for turn outs.'

'Do you ever think, Hughie, there are times when one should have a serious rethink?'

Hughie felt a surge of optimism, despite the mad idea regarding the study curtains. Fenn was sounding like herself again, positive and capable. She was peeling potatoes at great speed, sleeves pushed up to show her freckled forearms. There was an energy about her. That was what he'd always loved, her mixture of activity and tranquillity, a suppressed vitality, always waiting to spill over. The salad, already washed, and in a bowl, was, worryingly, liberally scattered with herbs. Hughie felt she was in charge. Fenn was going to reassess all the peculiar ideas she'd been fostering for most of the year, and come back into the fold of common sense. Home would be calm and safe once more.

'One should never be drastic,' said Hughie, 'and certainly not in the study.' He wondered if this were the moment to unburden himself. No need to mention the fleeting moment of lust. That was out of the question. Anyway, Hughie reluctantly acknowledged he wasn't adultery material. But Dodo's behaviour had become an irritation in his mind, which needed healing.

'You're like the study,' said Fenn. 'Neither of you ever change.'

'Stability is what I'm good at. I'm glad you're having a rethink, this church thing.'

'I never said that. I've had my rethink. It's your turn now.'

'Whatever would I rethink? I've retained values proven over the years. I do my very best at all times. What is there to change?'

'I want you to ask yourself questions. Not think the same as you did thirty years ago. About your inner self, for a start.'

'Has this got anything to do with the meditation thing? I knew anything to do with Dodo would be trouble.'

Fenn threw the potatoes into a pan, and clattered it under the tap. 'You're not listening to me, Hughie. I'd like to tell you about this afternoon, but I know you won't listen. Your ears will have muffs over them.'

She didn't add that Hughie was so rigid his soul might get rigor mortis. Nor did she say that if she confided in Lex, who was a confirmed atheist, she knew he'd listen.

Hughie edged in beside her at the sink, to get his hands under the tap. 'Yes, Dodo is trouble. She tried to get at me, you know.' He felt himself getting pink.

'Get at you? Have an argument?'

'Touch me.' Already, Hughie regretted he'd started.

'Touch you?'

Wincing, Hughie demonstrated what she'd done with her hand, running it down his front. 'So embarrassing.' He looked hopefully at Fenn, knowing she would understand he'd had no part in it. 'It was after the pheasant,' he added, by way of explanation.

Fenn looked at him, the saucepan in her hand. Slowly, she put it down, then leaned on the edge of the stove. Her shoulders started to wobble.

'You're not upset, are you?'

She stood, clinging to the stove, shoulders still shaking.

'You're not crying old thing, are you?' Tentatively he touched her arm.

Fenn turned round, and she could scarcely say for laughing, 'Hughie, I wish I'd been there.'

'She wouldn't have done it if you had been.' Hughie was hurt the encounter was cut down to size, sorry that Fenn hadn't got upset. 'I've got some marking. I'll be in the study.'

'Devious bitch,' said Fenn. The alien world loosed its hold, she was ruffled. The supply of generosity was abruptly cut off. She closed her eyes, dangling her fingers in the cold water among the potato peelings. Why did Hughie have to tell her that, why hadn't he protected her? Why was she always bandaging his knee? It may have been funny, but it was hurtful, too. Dodo was as frustrated as a bitch on heat, but she should never have gone for Hughie.

In the study, the cat was asleep under the bookcase behind the door. Hughie picked her up. 'Mysterium,' he whispered, 'comfort me. Purr to me.' The cat opened one eye and stared at him. Gradually, as if from nothing, her purr materialized, swelling to a crescendo of love, comforting and soothing him, though her green eyes, closed to a splinter of light, were inscrutable.

# Chapter Twelve

'What have you done to your hair?'

'Isn't it obvious?' Fenn and Dodo were in the client's kitchen, together with five cats, putting the last touches to the prawns in lemon and dill aspic. The cats watched silently, with uplifted faces. The kitchen was all white formica, challenging and clinical. The handles of the spoons and fish slice, hanging on the white tiled wall, were blood red.

'Remember,' said Fenn, 'this is not your opportunity to sparkle. Try to be as unobtrusive as possible.' She sounded cold, too remote to be even disapproving.

'It looks pretty. It's different,' said Dodo, and knew she'd got it wrong.

Fenn removed the clingfilm from the brown bread and butter, then ejected the cats, one by one, through the outside door. She looked very brisk in her white shirt, straight navy skirt, and shining wipe-over apron, decorated with drawings of vegetables. This she would remove, when she was ready to serve. Her hair, short and straight, no longer an ill-restrained bundle, but cut in a bob, swung confidently, as she moved about the kitchen.

Fenn had had it cut yesterday, because she needed to do something with all her energy. Hughie was devastated. 'Is it my fault?' he asked.

Dodo watched her. Fenn was in a funny mood. The arrangement for Dodo to help out was made weeks ago, before the pheasant supper. Hughie might have said something. To comfort herself, Dodo picked up what she took to be a stray prawn. Too late, she realized it was essential garnish.

'Dodo. We can't have eleven aspics with a prawn on top, and one naked.'

'Lemon peel,' suggested Dodo, 'in curls.'

'Do that then. I've got to finish the port sauce.'

Dodo hacked hopefully at the lemon and ate a couple more prawns, as they were no longer essential.

Fenn couldn't decide what best to do. On one hand, no harm had been done. Hughie had been scared out of his wits. She needed Dodo to help out at this lunch, and it would be stupid to have a bad atmosphere between them, bad for business. On the other hand, Dodo was a friend, and she'd tried to deceive her. Fenn wanted generosity to flow through her, to be relaxed about the incident, but it wasn't easy to feel generous towards Dodo.

'I'm impressed you should bother to do the full works with a pheasant the other week,' said Fenn, 'game chips and all.'

'Boil in a bag. And crisps.'

'Ah.'

Dodo ate another prawn. Would Fenn work out one couldn't over-cater with frozen single portions? She changed the subject.

'Doug's kept a low profile, thank heavens,' said Dodo.

'You should never have gone out with him,' said Fenn, 'a man like that.'

'A man like what?'

'With a pigtail at his age.'

'Young at heart,' said Dodo. 'What you mean is, common.'

'You're probably right. There are some people it's asking too much to love.' She looked pointedly at the smudges in the aspic where prawns had once decoratively sat, and felt better.

The meal started elegantly. The clients were a literary group, all female, meeting for an annual lunch. If the food went well, Fenn might get the monthly contract for soup and snacks. Although a modest item, soup had a good mark-up.

As befitted their image, the women were a touch bohemian, long skirts, a headband here, a monocle there, a pair of tennis shoes, black nail varnish. One good looking woman, wearing a black velvet tug-on hat with a cheeky brim, was surreptitiously smoking behind her handbag.

They spoke in low tones, commenting on the aspic, inviting the cats, who had reappeared through the french doors, to sit on their knees.

Fenn knew the exact moment to clear, and almost unnoticed, began to slide the plates off the table. Dodo started at the other side of the table. The hostess, Jessica, who was clearly older than she thought she was, had only eaten half her lunch. She was eating half of everything at the moment, dieting, to get back her lover. A large ginger feline luxuriated on her knee, enjoying the sensation of her velvet trousers. It seemed sensible to Dodo, to give the cat the chance to finish off the prawns, and it chomped up what was left on the plate, without moving from the velvet knee.

'You like cats?' Jessica purred herself, in a carefully cultivated husky voice. 'A love of cats is as essential as a love of literature, to be complete. Darling, you must look after us another time.'

In the kitchen, Fenn said, 'Don't do that again, please Dodo. Letting animals lick plates isn't what I'm about.'

'It made the old girl's day. I've probably got you a contract. You heard her say come another time.'

'All the same,' said Fenn, and let it go at that.

Fenn served the tenderloin noisettes girded in spinach, on a purée of celeriac, and Dodo followed with the new potatoes. She found co-ordinating a serving spoon and fork in one hand difficult, often needing a finger, to shove a reluctant tuber in the right direction.

Jessica said to the guest with black nail varnish, 'I loathed this month's novel. It was almost an Aga saga. Did you choose it for us?'

'Better than the pretentious American rubbish you made us read.'

'It certainly sorted the sheep from the goats,' Jessica purred.

'The trouble with the Booker committee is they never pick the winner,' said the woman with huge chestnut eyes, and drinking camomile tea, instead of wine.

'I've never been the same since I tripped over that camel,' said a small, grey-haired woman with a long nose and short front teeth.

'I don't think you can beat Jeffrey Archer,' said Dodo, joining in. 'I like a good read myself.' She moved, to ask Jessica if she'd read his latest, and stepped on a tabby with three bells round its neck.

It ran shrieking and tinkling under the table. Five guests dived under the cloth to comfort it.

When Fenn dropped Dodo off, she went to see May in the flat below. She had another letter from Damaris, and May always liked to hear the latest. Fenn was still feeling annoyed, but for new reasons.

'To top it all, Dodo poured coffee over a woman in black jeans and Mao tunic. It went all the way down into her gym shoe. She walked out to the kitchen squelching at one end, and blaspheming at the other. I think that

125

was the final straw. There was no mention of further business.'

'Poor Dodo,' said May.

'Poor Fenn, more like. It's my business she was wrecking.' It was impossible to forgive Dodo, impossible to feel calm, or generous.

'That's Dodo for you. I'm glad you popped in, dear.'

'Do you find it hard to love your neighbour, May?'

'I keep trying.'

'I think it's asking altogether too much. The most you can do is ignore some of them. Let them be. But you can't love them. Take Doug as an example.'

'Doug is difficult, I agree.'

'I'm trying very hard to let generosity overflow onto Doug, but there's a blockage. I try, then he knocks some more paint off the skirting, or belches, and it's gone.'

'Are you trying to get back.'

'Get back?'

'I'm talking about the church,' May, sitting in her wing chair, in a shaft of sunlight, looked perky with anticipation. 'I've prayed for this, you know, Fenn.'

Fenn was gentle, tried not to think that May was a silly old trout who couldn't get her mind round the possibility that her entire faith was a myth. 'I'm sorry, May.'

May sighed. It had not yet come to pass, the saving of Fenn.

'I came to tell you we've had another letter from Damaris. It quite surprises me how often she writes. I'll just read you the bit about you.'

'I'd like to see all of it. You know how fond I am of her, how close we've always been.'

'I don't think you'd be interested in all of it, May, dear.'

'Is it private?'

126

'Well, no.'

'Please.'

Reluctantly, Fenn handed over the sheets of airmail.

Dear Mum and Dad,

Thanks for your letter Mum. Nice to know everything is going on as always. We're still in Sydney after all. There was a bit of a do after a party, and we were held up.

Life is great out here. So is Eric. I met him in the police station. He's definitely not HIV, and anyway, he's changing his orientation. It's wonderful to know someone who has so much alternative experience. He looks a real hunk.

Getting jobs is still difficult. We're thinking of going for the grape picking. Don't worry about the red necks. Eric says he'll guard me with his life. Mind you, it might be me having to guard Eric with mine. It took me ages to realize this Aussie hadn't got the name wrong when he came up to Eric and said, 'Are you Guy?' Anyway, he's had his hair cut since then.

This week there's been a washing-up job. Greasy cold water and tea towels the colour of mud.

Don't tell Dodo, but Marie is getting Buddhist tendencies. She and this huge bloke, Boris, sit in the park with their legs crossed and eyes closed, and meditate every evening. That's what she says they do, anyway.

Tell May I love her. I could do with some of her salmon mousse right now, or those little scones. Eating on the bread line is the hardest part.

Don't worry, Dad, about me. I'm fine. I miss your nagging, Mum. Must go now because Eric wants to go window shopping.

All my love,

Damaris

'Nice to know she still thinks about me,' said May, 'but she's got some funny friends.'

'You know how she exaggerates,' said Fenn. 'I hope she does.'

After supper Fenn went into the garden, breathing deep of the early summer air. She felt ruffled by Dodo, and now more ruffled by having exposed Damaris's current life style to May. She'd intended only to comfort her by showing May she was thought about. Hughie was petulant because the exams were coming up.

She sat under the willow. Leaning up against the trunk, she closed her eyes and tried to imagine all the irritations falling away from her. She sought the generosity of the earth, and the alien light she had seen at the meditation class. She listened to the sound of birds in the early evening, and watched the last rays of the sun. She was aware that in the tree trunk behind her life was rising up from the earth.

The great burden of having to love the deeply unlovable seemed too much this evening. She made her face relax, and she smiled, a sad smile of resignation. Peace was as elusive as God had been.

Hughie looked out of the study window and sighed. He didn't like to see his wife sitting under a tree, half her hair gone, and smiling to herself like that. It wasn't sensible. He wondered what she was smiling about.

'Dear God,' he said, 'please make Fenn normal again, and make her hair grow quickly.'

Fenn came inside when the phone rang. Hughie wasn't fond of the telephone and never felt any sense of urgency about knowing who was ringing.

'Hello.'

'It's Pru.' She sounded distraught.

'Anything the matter?'

'It's Gareth. I told you about him.'

128

'From fossils?'

'He took me to the cinema twice. Then his wife came round, and tried to beat me up.'

'Pru. How awful for you. Are you badly hurt?'

'Not a single bru . . . ise . . .' The sound of her sobs were exaggerated by the phone. Fenn absent-mindedly wiped the instrument with her handkerchief.

'Do you want me to come down to you?'

'There's no need. I'm all right. It's just that nothing ever goes right for me.'

'I know, Pru, and you do deserve it to go right. Did you like him a lot?'

'Not any more. What am I going to do? Is anything every going to go right for me?'

'One day, Pru. I'm sure it will one day. Remember the Chinese proverb. Keep a green bough in your heart, and the singing bird will come.'

'It's hard enough when you've got faith, I don't think I can manage the Orient just now. Anyway, I've got to go now, Fenn. French homework to do.'

# Chapter Thirteen

That was the roses dead-headed. Her yellow shrub, Mrs-something-or-other, was always the first to come, and the first to go over. The bushes were like lassies coming out of the hairdressers, all fresh and tidy round the head.

May wore her gardening apron, with its useful pocket, in which she now put the secateurs. She took up her bucket and moved to the small tidy compost heap. Bucket by bucket, she mulched the border, tucking melting leaf mould round delphiniums and lupins, to prolong their lives. She caressed the small pinks, delicate-looking, but as strong as horses. Pinks she grew, but not carnations, especially not yellow ones. It would be more than she could bear, to have such a reminder of Lewis always there in her garden. Always three, he gave her, three yellow carnations. She spread more round the Japanese anemones and michs to come, so that they would become healthy autumn flowers.

She noticed the clematis Montana was getting rampant. Keeping chaos at bay is what gardening is all about. Nature is a wonderful thing, but it has to be controlled, if you're going to have a garden. Like life. That's always on the brink of breaking down, unless you keep a very wary watch.

She went to the shed to get the secateurs. They

weren't there. She paused, thinking, now I must not be unchristian, but my mind goes first to Doug. She'd asked him to mow the lawn on Thursday, and he didn't seem to think it came into his cleaning job. So he might have taken those things out of spite. He'd been just as difficult when she'd forgotten to pay him, because of not going to the bank. She would have suggested he gave her a lift there, but she didn't fancy driving in that van. Funny about the van. She'd thought she'd seen Dodo in it once as she'd done her shopping. Another little sign of the mind being unreliable, she supposed.

As a reward for her hard afternoon's work, she made some cucumber sandwiches and a pot of tea which she carried into the garden. She put them on the wrought-iron table she'd got when Auntie Elfie died. They'd had a very big garden, though rather formal. She fetched a kitchen chair to sit on. Then, dear Hughie appeared, tippy-toeing round from the back entrance, as if he were afraid to alarm her.

'I'll fetch another cup,' she said.

'Let me,' said Hughie, 'or shall I bring out another chair?'

When they were comfortably settled, Hughie said gently, 'I had a letter from Mellowstones this morning.' Hughie glanced up at the top floor window, and thought he saw Lex turning away. He wasn't completely certain. It was uncomfortable to think that creature might have been spying on him. He took his attention back to May.

She stroked her fingers across the table, as if trying to smooth out a non-existent cloth.

'Do you want me to tell you what it says?'

'Not really.'

'We're thinking a long way into the future, May. Planning is only an insurance.'

'I'm being silly, aren't I? Running away. Yes, of

131

course you must read me the letter. So kind of you to bother with all this.'

'I can assure you Mellowstones is not an institutional sort of place at all.'

'But, Hughie dear, it won't be you in it.'

Hughie firmed up his voice. 'They say that to secure a place any time in the next two years, we must put your name down now. That's not to say there's a two-year waiting list exactly. You see, people become ready at different times, not necessarily in the expected order. And others, er, well, they leave.'

'I understand. Yes.'

'So would you like me to . . .'

'I may not be able to afford it.'

'Now for the good news. There are some second floor rooms which aren't suitable for most of the guests. The stairs are too much, and the lift only goes to the first floor. But you're particularly spry. No problem for you, May. The prices are very good.' He handed over a tariff.

'Will they be little poky cupboards which were maids' rooms?' Her neck seemed to sink into her shoulders like a nesting owl.

Hughie felt pleased he'd done a thorough job. 'Absolutely not. I've done a personal inspection. They were the day and night nurseries. Really big. South facing, so you can see right over to the church. Nicely furnished, but the Matron said they can always move some of the furniture out, to make room for any special pieces of your own.'

'The day nursery. Of course. I've seen it, you know. Fenn took me to the sale preview. Dodo fell off the rocking horse.' May could imagine the rattan table sitting lonely and out of place next to the institution bed with stiff white sheets. The bed would be hard and narrow. Undoubtedly the loo, any loo, would always be occupied when she was ready to go.

'Thank you, Hughie. I don't really know what to do for the best. I'm not really ready.'

'Exactly. But what harm in having your name down, just in case?' Hughie glanced up again at the window of the top flat. No-one was there now.

'I'll have to think about it.' May set out the cups, poured out the milk. She gently inclined the teapot, and out came a steady stream of clear water.

Lex looked out of his window, down into the back garden, and saw May having tea with Hughie. Inside, the room was stuffy and he was at a loose end. He hadn't realized how much of his time he had managed to use up, writing the book. He went down the stairs, and let himself out of the front door.

Fenn lay under the weeping willow. The sunlight dappled her face and hair through the breathing curtain of leaves, caressing and comforting. The sun caught the lurking red lights in her hair, hints of rainbow fires, dancing.

Before breakfast, it had rained when the sun was out, healing, and joyful rain. Although the grass was now dry, there still was water in a puddle beside the lawn, reflecting each murmur of the trees, each whim of the breeze, always moving, always reflecting movement, ever changing.

The grass was quite long, daisies had appeared, perky and certain of themselves. Fenn decided to let the grass grow for as long as Hughie would tolerate, so that she could swish through it with bare feet, and there would be not only daisies, but ladies smock and trefoils as well.

She lay with her hands across her stomach and felt the air as it ebbed and flowed through her. The pace of her breathing slowed and the tension drifted away.

She felt the stream of life washing past and saw her problems float away. Except that it was impossible to let Damaris float away. What was she getting into now? What had happened to the pretty little seven-year-old with her hair braided in a single plait, always so eager to please?

The air was healing. It was kindly and gentle. She was able to visualize the white light, which is the energy of life, as it seemed to suffuse the world. Eventually she felt more at one with the nature around her, with the breathing of the earth, with the throb of its life. Fenn considered Damaris. She hoped that the purity of the light would link with Damaris's own spirit, that somehow . . .

She sighed. It doesn't work like that. She was trying to make something happen. It was like praying. She knew she shouldn't be trying to force her wishes to come true, but seeking the harmony that had to be listened for, searching for the oneness of the earth. Through that would come the healing balance.

Fenn went indoors to make some mint tea. While she was waiting for the water to boil, she tore up all the garden plans that she had kept over the years: old catalogues, lists, computer printouts, and articles from magazines. They went into the dustbin. She switched on the computer and deleted the files of weekly garden tasks and lists of vegetables rotations. She unloosed the girding around the life of the garden. She set it free.

She took the tea outside and sat on the wooden seat, under the kitchen window, on the paved area, and listened to the birds singing. They were especially vibrant.

The smells of mint and lovage reached her from the tubs. Where, she wondered, do all lovely smells go? Do they become so widely dispersed that they are not available to an ordinary nose? Perhaps, though, they are always there, open to the sensitive spirit, peace-giving, and healing.

'Hello? Is Hughie about?' Lex walked through the back gate. He was unhealthily pale, and his shirt was large and baggy.

'Oh. You,' said Fenn, and pulled herself together. 'He's gone to see May.'

'I'd wanted a word with him, really. See if he thinks there's any chance of a permanent post at St Anthony's.'

'I imagine they're hoping Woodhouse will be back. Why would you want to stay at St Anthony's?'

'It has the odd advantage. Of course, they'd prefer Woodhouse back, wouldn't they? He always toed the line.'

'I'm afraid he did. Look where that got him. His medication has been cut down quite a bit now, though.'

Lex nodded and sat on the other end of the bench, as if prepared to wait for Hughie's return.

'What have you been up to, Lex? Haven't seen you about.'

'That's not exactly my fault, is it?'

'Still doing your philosophy discussions?'

'Absolutely.' Lex leaned towards her. 'They're going well. The answer to everything. To convince you might take some time. Ages and ages. Perhaps we could have tea together during the week? You can't say no to tea. Easily the safest meal there is.' He moved up along the seat. His knee was almost touching hers. She could feel its warmth across the space. Fenn noticed that there was a hole in the elbow of his shirt.

'I'll give you tea now. Hughie will be back any minute.'

'Not much point,' said Lex. He grimaced, accepting defeat. 'As you say, Woodhouse will be returning. I've got things to do.' He was about to stand up when Hughie walked into the garden.

'Hello,' said Lex. 'I've come round to see you, actually. But Fenn's answered the question. It was about Woodhouse coming back.'

'Almost recovered,' said Hughie. 'Certain to be back soon.'

'I'll be off then.'

'I'll see you out.'

Fenn sat down again, and closed her eyes. She could still feel the warmth of Lex, close to her.

'You could have caught me at May's. In fact, I thought you might have seen me,' said Hughie, at the gate. Lex had looked much too at home on that bench, and sitting far too close to Fenn.

'Obviously not,' said Lex, 'otherwise . . .' He walked off. He really had thought she might agree to tea.

## Chapter Fourteen

'Feeling our age are we, Mrs Lomax?' said Doug when he found May sitting at the kitchen table with a cup of coffee, exactly where he'd left her half an hour before. Suddenly, moved by a chance pang of compassion, he added, 'You're OK, aren't you?'

'Thank you, Doug, I'm in excellent health, as always.' There was no reason to drop one's standards now, by gossiping with the servants.

Doug made himself a mug of coffee, added four spoons of sugar, and sat down opposite. May winced. But, of course, she must remember that Doug was not a servant. He was an entrepreneur and perfectly equal. It was unchristian to think otherwise. She made herself smile at him, but was glad the biscuits were not out. She didn't fancy watching Doug chomping on a chocolate digestive. He'd talk with it in his mouth and spit out crumbs.

'Your mother keeping well?' she asked. That he lived with his mother was all she knew of his personal life.

'Liver playing her up a bit this morning. I tell her to watch it, but she says she likes to keep it well exercised. It was given her to digest booze, and she doesn't like to think of it lying idle.'

'I've never really liked drink myself,' mused May, 'especially not sherry.'

'You're doing OK, Mrs L.' Doug was pleased she didn't immediately get up from the table when he sat down. Her disdain was not a quivering aura of disapproval this morning. She wasn't a bad old stick really, just a bleeding snob.

'I'm not so sure I'm doing OK at all. You see . . .'

Doug raised his eyebrows in what appeared to be sympathy, but was really to encourage revelation.

'I'm . . . I'm on the waiting list.'

'Aren't we all, Mrs L. Waiting for that last trumpet, as you might say.'

'No, the one before the last, I hope. Mellowstones.'

'Cost you a bomb.'

May recoiled. It had been unwise to disclose her problem to this man, but discuss money she would not.

'It would be a room with a view,' she said, 'because I'm particularly spry.'

'Ma's spry, when she's not legless. Being in a place like that might knock her into shape, do you think? They'd want her back before eleven, I imagine.'

'Your mother would find a place like that extremely dull,' said May. 'I expect the inmates have orgies of knitting pattern swapping. I don't expect to find it particularly stimulating myself.'

'Ma would liven it up. She'd give 'em all a new lease of life. Bring back a little gleam of hope to those watery old eyes. Reach the parts they thought had been pruned.'

'I take it you're talking about men. The ones I've seen are beyond all that.'

'Beyond what, Mrs L?' Doug smirked unpleasantly at her discomfort.

May bit her tongue. She refused to discuss money with the likes of Doug, and now she nearly got onto sex. 'Would you beeswax the dining table today, please,' she said quickly.

'Trouble with all this old stuff, it doesn't come up nice, without nearly breaking your wrist.'

May stayed at the kitchen table, imagining long conversations about the weather, and petty television rivalries, and bland food chosen for its digestibility. She sniffed vigorously, to suck some of the water back from under her eyelids.

The mahogany came up particularly well that morning because as Doug battled with his duster he saw, like a vision, how he could get his revenge on the likes of Mrs L and Fenn Meadowcroft, and that doss-bag Dodo, who all thought they were above him, and did so little to disguise it. They were, after all, only the middle classes, not the aristocracy, whose repugnance he'd have found easy to forgive. A lesser man would have dreamed of rape, or public humiliation, but Doug was subtle. Doug knew where the pain would be the most excruciating for this little old lady, dreading that life would not run out before her dwindling income. Doug would use his mother. Not only would her keep be assured, he'd give her a booze allowance as well. A generous one. Fenn Meadowcroft would be dancing mad.

Doug named his cleaning firm Vroom for good reason. He believed in moving fast, like a rocket, getting to where he wanted in a hurry.

It was with unrestrained triumph that he walked into Fenn's kitchen two weeks later. 'Have I left my mobile with you?' he asked. 'I put it down somewhere.'

'I don't think you have,' said Fenn. She was disorganized because Hughie had been in a state over the A-levels arriving at school. He dreaded the boys coming to find out their results personally.

'Must be in the office then. Never mind. Poor Mrs Lomax is going in, she tells me,' he said.

'Mrs Lomax deserves some pampering,' said Fenn. '*Anno Domini* has caught up with her.'

'Like with Ma.' Doug did not bustle on, but hovered, in black leather, looking like a carrion crow.

'What's Ma done now?'

'She propositioned the Vicar,' said Doug with barely concealed pride. 'He came round to see me, and said it would be better for everyone if she was in some sort of protective environment. I thought he was going to say protective custody, but he couldn't have known about the other, I decided.'

'What other?'

'That bust up with the neighbour, over playing loud music at one in the morning.'

'Can't say I blame her,' said Fenn. 'Most inconsiderate of them.'

'It was Ma playing the music. Guns and Roses, her favourite group.'

'What sort of protection are you giving her? Or are you laying on some sort of protection for the Vicar?'

Doug recognized his moment. 'Done the only thing I could do. Put her in Mellowstones.' He ranged his small eyes over Fenn, judging her dismay, searching for unlikely signs of admiration, or better still, jealousy.

'It's very expensive,' said Fenn severely.

'Easy come, easy go,' said Doug. 'I've just picked up a nice little earner from the Education Committee. Had to take on more staff. Money for old rope. Give me local government any day.'

Fenn didn't let her dismay show, but plans for May's tranquil and refined twilight had not included the likes of Mrs Doug. She would provide an evil focus from which May would be unable to avert her gaze. Her excesses would be a perpetual torment, her crudeness a measure of what May felt her desserts to be.

'She's in the night nursery because she's spry enough.

Its previous inmate had a perf. Very suitable for Ma. Queen of the night, Pa used to call her.'

'A perf?'

'Perforated duodenal ulcer. Kept a bottle in her room, I believe.' Doug walked into the hall with a flourish of his pigtail and Fenn leaned up against the back door.

Two minutes later the phone rang. Fenn took the call in the kitchen. 'Could I speak to my father, please? It's Murray.' His voice was flat and, at the same time, clearly anxious. She knew what he was ringing about. Hughie had gone out that very morning, bracing himself against such disappointment.

Fenn tactfully moved into the hall. If Doug hadn't shouted she would never have heard him say, 'You can't have missed the sodding grades. You're going to Oxford. What am I going to tell the bloody clients?'

# Chapter Fifteen

Lex lay in bed, staring at the window and the grey sky he could see beyond. He turned over, pulled his knees up high, and pretended he had flu, and the bedroom had a glowing fire. He imagined the ache in his back and legs being soothed by the warmth, and that he was slowly drifting into a happy doze. It was his most comforting fantasy; it took him back to when he was eight-years-old. The only time his mother had really taken any notice of him was when he was ill. He'd been put in her room and the electric fire, which had simulated flames, was switched on low.

Not that he needed to wallow in self-pity over his mother's lack of maternal support. He owed more than most to Granpy. He could bake cakes, and there was always something special in the tin whenever Lex went round to his house, chocolate fudge or damp lemon sponge, raisin bars, or cinnamon fingers. Looking back, it was strange that Granpy had never taught him to cook, he had taught him so much else.

Lex knew the postman had come, the footstep on the gravel path was a sound he listened for every day with childlike optimism. He pulled on jeans and a sweater over his pyjamas in case he met Dodo on the stairs. She might take nightwear as an invitation.

He wished he hadn't got up when he saw the envelope. It was A4, brown and addressed in his own handwriting. Slowly he returned to the upstairs flat, though going faster on the middle landing. Safe behind his closed front door, he leaned with his head against the glass, looking out at the grey morning and feeling sick in the area below the ribcage.

Coffee. He needed coffee. But there wasn't any. He needed a shoulder on which to lay his weary head, and comforting arms around him that smelled of very fresh, but not sweet, flowers. There'd be a fortune made with a scent catching the spring earthiness of wet early narcissi. This fair creature would cook for him, bacon and shiny fried bread, which would take away that empty feeling in his soul, as well as stomach. He wondered whether the decline in proper cooking was linked to the decline in religion. In his case, yes. It was strange how meals came into all religions: dietary laws, last suppers, pockets of rice, pork phobia.

In the absence of both woman and delicious consumables, he breakfasted on a mug of packet soup and a Mars bar. It wasn't until he finished, and was feeling much worse that he could bring himself to open the envelope and read the letter which came with the returned manuscript.

He knew they would. They had. They'd got hold of the wrong end of the stick. Who were publishers, after all? People who wanted to be in the book world, but couldn't write? 'Not quite professional enough,' they said. Well, it wasn't meant for professional philosophers. It was aimed at the ordinary man. It was a book of ideas for strictly non-philosophers to philosophize about. Idiots. He supposed, thinking about it, he'd known all the time that this would happen. But what devil had driven him to spend so many hours working on it, to alienate so many people at St Anthony's in testing out the arguments? He knew the answer to that as well. Answers come easier on grey days, it's a good light in which to see the truth. He'd done it because he wanted to make his mark, to have his ideas count. It was not a muse prompting him, but his own engorged pride.

There it sat, the text potentially to change lives, its edges battered only by being stuffed uncaringly back into the envelope, not by hands eager for knowledge. I know the type, decided Lex, who read that so carelessly. Sidesman on a Sunday. High Tory. Secretly wishes he could write like Jeffrey Archer. Oxbridge degree in English. 'Sod you,' he said.

When he felt a bit stronger, when the polyglutinates had ceased to clash with the cholesterol, he would go out and buy two more A4 envelopes, and the right stamps, and today's paper. Also some proper food. Sausages, perhaps? For the short term he made do with Friday's paper which he hadn't properly read.

He turned away from the horoscope. In rejecting a higher power, he had asserted the right to make his own destiny. Sitting in a top floor flat on a grey Saturday was not getting very far with making his own destiny.

What could he do about it? He fancied a married woman who made it clear there was nothing on. He was certain he'd detected, on those sensitive antennae which have given guidance and encouragement to man since he accepted his first apple, that she was indeed conscious of his presence in a special way. Lex sighed, he doubted he would ever be able to do anything about Fenn Meadowcroft, or shape his own destiny.

Only by chance did he turn idly to page fourteen, and he saw it, the advertisement, tucked away modestly in the bottom right-hand corner. It was for a post in New Zealand, in a school which was experimenting with using philosophy as a teaching method.

\*　　　\*　　　\*

The post had arrived when Fenn went downstairs to make some tea. There was one envelope in Damaris's typical scrawl. The postmark told her the letter was posted the day after Fenn lay under the willow tree, and tried to be in tune with Damaris's soul.

Dearest Mum and Dad,
    Marie and I are travelling alone, well with two other girls, but they're not very interesting. I'm writing this in a heavenly place on the bank of a stream. We're just outside Adelaide. It's a bit cold, but I've bought a new jacket.
    Marie has found a little bird, which looks pretty sick, and is trying to fetch it some water. We haven't any vessels with us, and she's trying to carry water in her cupped hands. Every time she gets back to the bird, the water has seeped away. Personally, I think the bird looks worse now, with all this swooping about over it.
    Tomorrow, I'm going to see that relative of yours, Ray, in hospital.

Fenn couldn't believe there was no mention of Eric, no mention of any weird men at all. She sat at the kitchen table in her towelling dressing gown and read the letter three times. She warmed her fingers round her mug of tea and stared out into the garden at the pearl light of the morning, which had washed the earth clean. Eventually, she took some tea up to Hughie. She sat on the bed while he drank it and read out the letter to him.

'She's going to see Ray,' Fenn told him. 'I think it'll upset her. Just a few years older than she is, and with no real future. I'll never stop thinking of him, you know. Lying there, in a hospital bed. He won't even know she's there, will he?'

Hughie preferred not to contemplate the tragedy and got out of bed without saying anything.

Fenn was reluctant to let go of the letter. She took it downstairs and read it again. While she was cupping her hands, as if to carry water, in sympathy with Marie, the phone rang. Fenn grabbed it. People don't make social calls at seven o'clock in the morning.

'Hello. You don't know me, but my name's Mrs Penfold. I'm Pru's neighbour. I'm in the flat next to hers, though not at the moment. I'm using her telephone because I'm not on it.'

'Something's happened?'

'I thought you should be told. She's in hospital just now.'

'Whatever for? She wasn't ill a day or two ago.'

'I'm sure she's perfectly all right really. It must have been an accident. She hadn't even taken the whole bottle, there were quite a few pills left. I thought I'd tell you, because it's not my responsibility, after all. She came round to me in a bit of a panic, in the middle of the night. I'd only just got off.'

'Thank you, Mrs Penfold. I'll come immediately.'

'I'm sorry to have troubled you.'

Pru was in a four-bedded ward, where no-one was speaking to her because they didn't know how to deal with the pain that had led her there, and didn't want to risk making matters worse. She was shrouded in a hospital gown, worn back to front, coming high up under her chin, making her look like a vicar. Her face was almost the same colour as the pillow, and she clung on to a kidney bowl, lying on the sheet beside her.

Fenn sat by the bed, put the dish on the bedside locker, and took her hand. 'Pru. I didn't understand how it was.'

Pru stared at her gratefully. 'I couldn't sleep so I took some pills. I forgot. Still couldn't sleep. They muddled me, so I must have taken some more. Sorry.'

'Is that really what happened?'

'Yes, of course it's what happened. Anyway, how did you know?'

'Mrs Penfold rang.'

'Interfering old bag.'

The Ward Sister appeared, looking stressed. 'And you are?'

'I'm Pru's sister.'

'Back from the dead, eh? She told us, no living relatives.'

'I was confused,' said Pru, her eyes fixed on the bowl on the locker, as if it were some sort of refuge.

'Would it be possible for me to take her home?' asked Fenn, working to keep her voice steady. She wasn't certain whether she was more hurt by Pru's denial of sister, or upset by the lack of compassion in a member of the caring profession.

'Doctor's round at eleven. I imagine she'll be discharged. Leave that bowl alone, dear. There's nothing left in your stomach.'

Pru started to cry. Sister clucked her tongue, and moved on to the next bed.

Fenn silently cradled her sister. Pru whispered, 'I didn't want you to know.'

'I should have seen. I'm so sorry, Pru. I really am.'

Driving home made it easier to talk. There's a lack of eye contact if one person is at the wheel.

'I've tried so hard, Fenn. All I seem to do is evening classes. Sometimes coffee with a girl from the office. Mavis. But she's such a spinster. Like me. I'm a spinster, aren't I?'

'You're only thinking like that because you're down. No-one's on the shelf, as they used to say, because there are always new people coming along these days. Broken marriages. Recycled opportunities.' Fenn had never

147

before considered the advantages of a high divorce rate.

'I hate the office now. All the others are so young. Discuss their brand of pill. Skirts about an inch short of nothing. Hair always tangled up, never clean looking.'

'You could change the job. You're well qualified. Got experience.'

'That won't change my life, will it? Always alone. Never living for someone else.'

After leaving the hospital, they went to the flat to collect clothes. As Pru packed in the bedroom Fenn made some tea. She waited for the kettle to boil and looked round at the shelf of recipe books, meals crying out to be cooked with love, at eight plants on the window sill, flourishing, tended like children, and at the framed posters and prints. These were of country kitchens, groups of cane chairs in a garden, children on a 1920s beach, all faces of family life. Pru's companions, as she dangled her single tea bag in her late-night drinking mug. Fenn could see how very much Pru needed to live for someone else.

They'd put the eight plants in the boot, with the suitcase.

'Why not move down to us? At least there's always family near by.' Fenn paused while she overtook a lorry that was churning out smoke. 'As it happens, May's moving out of her flat quite soon, and I happen to know the Head's secretary is leaving at the end of term. Hughie could put in a word for you. It might save them all the bother of interviewing.'

'London is such a fun place,' said Pru, automatically. She rested her head back on the support and half closed her eyes, looking at the lowering sun as they drove west. Had God, at last, at long last, come to see her needs, she wondered. Slowly, the tears slid down her face, not tears of pain, but of relief. Fenn hadn't said one word of reproach.

As Pru dozed beside her, Fenn planned how to break it gently to Hughie that Pru would be staying with them for a while. They'd have tea in the study among the books and the unbanishable smell of dust. She'd light a fire there. It would launder the air, sucking it up the chimney. She might even move the telly in.

They left the motorway and moved through quieter roads where the fields on either side were drained of their summer lushness, except where there was fresh plough land. Fenn wound down the window and let in the smell of the earth as it rushed by, damp and pungent.

She may have organized Pru's journey from the flat, as she'd organized everything in the past, calm and efficient. This time, it would be different. She'd offer, but she wouldn't shape. She must allow Pru to grow. Hughie, too. She must allow those close to her to be themselves, to make their own identity. She must deny her own need to impose. Her gift would be space, empty of herself, space to heal.

As the sisters drove through the quiet afternoon it was as if they swam together in a warm light, laughing as children.

# Chapter Sixteen

Hughie picked up the cat who'd been sleeping peacefully under the radiator and pulled her close to his chest. She settled herself on his knee. She felt very warm, very warm indeed. Pru had been with them three days. She was almost back to her usual self. She cooked yesterday's supper, liver. Hughie was averse to liver, on account of the tubes you get in it. Apparently Pru had bought the stuff before Fenn could warn her. There was a raspberry jam and custard tart to follow. It looked like a wound gone septic.

'Mysterium,' he whispered, 'tell Hughie what to do. You know everything. You see into people's hearts, don't you? That woman will drive me to the brink.' He'd escaped into the study when he came home. Even there, one of the spider plants that had arrived with Pru was dangling from a book shelf and tickling his neck.

Mysterium sat, aloof and uncaring, looking into his eyes at the reflection there of her beautiful self.

'All knowing one, Fenn won't suggest Pru stays forever, will she?'

The cat blinked once, lazy, insolent.

'Is that a yes or a no?'

If only Pru was all there was to worry him. Why should he have been put out when he found Lex sitting on the garden seat? He had no need to be, but he was.

Fenn's garden seat. He'd bought it for her specially, to prepare vegetables in the summer, instead of in the kitchen. There Fenn had consorted with the enemy. Not consorted exactly, but . . . Lex should never have been there in the first place.

On top of that were the results. The As hadn't been too bad, considering the collective IQ was about half that of a field mouse. It just showed what could be done by teaching in the form of model exam answers. It was the GCSEs that upset him. The set which the toad Lex taught got a hundred per cent pass rate, and they were the second stream. There were even five grade As, including a star. The best results the school ever had. In Hughie's own set, the top stream, seven had got a miserable E, and there was nothing above B.

'Mysterium,' he murmured, burying his chin in her neck fur. Mysterium pulled her head away, and looked at him coldly. It was not, after all, a mealtime. The cat was quiet lately, sleeping most of the time, or lying, staring moodily into space. 'Cat goddess of old Nile, a lot of help you are. Incapable of engaging with real life. Like me, I suppose.' He gathered her up to hug her, for comfort, and that was when he felt the lump. It was large and solid, a tight, uncompromising lump on her left flank, just below the spine.

'God,' said Hughie. 'Don't let it be.'

Mysterium scrambled off his knee, and returned to beneath the radiator.

Fortunately the vet's surgery was still going on, so Hughie took her along without making an appointment.

He came back, white-faced, holding the cat basket protectively to him. Slowly, he opened it to let Mysterium flow out, her tail juddering with annoyance.

'The vet's coming here. In the morning,' Hughie said. 'I won't have her die on a formica table.'

'They can't operate?' Fenn stared at the cat, not believing what she heard.

'Impossible. He was surprised the pain hasn't got to her yet.'

'We don't want her to be in pain.'

'She must be in her own domain, her own kingdom, and among her own people. He's going to cremate her. I couldn't bear to think of her rotting down, in the garden.'

Waiting for the vet to arrive, Hughie held Mysterium, and she struggled, rigid and resentful. He felt the muscles of her neck against his cheek, and the way her backside fitted exactly into his hand. He stroked her paws which were like silver pussy willow tufts. He smelt the smell of her, like washing, fresh from the garden line. She hadn't purred all morning, though usually when picked up, she would gurgle into his ear. He closed his eyes, and committed the touch of her to his memory for ever. Fenn gave her smoked salmon for breakfast.

When the vet arrived, Hughie felt tempted to pretend they were out. Fenn opened the door, and said the study was the place to go. Hughie put her on a cushion on the sofa.

When the injection took effect, Hughie put his head down and from the warm, soft, compact body came a small, contented purr, so slight, that Hughie was never certain again that he'd actually heard it.

Mysterium slept, still warm, and her eyes gleamed with a clear green light, for a cat doesn't close its eyes in death. Fenn brought the blanket from the basket to wrap her in. 'A plastic bag wouldn't be right,' she said.

They took her out to the vet's hatchback and laid the blanket parcel next to two black plastic bags, each tied in a resolute knot. Hughie felt proud that Mysterium, warm in her own possession, was seen, so obviously, to be loved.

Mysterium, being a huge ego, left a void out of all proportion to her actual size and position in the hierarchy of the animal kingdom. For days, everywhere, her shadow leaped. She appeared in corners of the garden, at the foot of the stairs, under the kitchen table. Her ever presence created in Hughie a greater sense of loss, prompting the need to feel her small, argumentative body nestling against his neck.

At night, Hughie thought his heart would break. Fenn lay beside him and said, 'I'm certain Mysterium had a soul.'

'Where do you think it's gone?'

'Not to some yucky cats' paradise. Nothing twee. She'd wreck the place.'

'You can't cheer me up like that. It's as if she's still here.'

'I know. I think she is. Not quite ready to leave yet, because you loved her so much.'

'Do you think so? A little cat ghost?'

'Not quite like that. But part of the one spirit, that we all are. She's not quite lost her earth identity yet.'

'So she could always be there?'

'I think so. Yes.'

'We weren't taught that.'

'No.'

Hughie, for the first time, thought it might be possible to know such things here and now and not wait until he got to heaven himself, to check out the facts.

Fenn and Pru sat under the apple tree on a blanket, making the most of the autumn sun, and eating watercress sandwiches.

'I'm a lot of trouble, especially with Hughie so upset about the cat,' said Pru. 'I must be. I still don't know what I should do.'

Fenn was surprised she didn't automatically assure Pru she was no trouble at all, and give her a detailed list of what she herself would do. That would be give up the boring London job, and get fixed up to move into May's flat as soon as she left.

Instead, she looked across the grass at the Japanese anemones swaying on the breath of the autumn air, and felt the ephemerality of the peace of the afternoon as something that could never be formalized, or grasped ferociously.

She turned her head, and looked at her sister. 'It will come right, Pru. Give it time. You'll know what to do, soon.'

'If God would only help me, I could be so happy.'

'I don't know about God,' said Fenn. 'But know that we love you, Pru.'

'Hughie said that the Head's secretary job hasn't been advertised yet.'

'So there's no hurry.'

'I like it here,' said Pru, and leaned back against the tree, tilting her head to catch the last of the sun. She'd been wounded, and now she was being healed. It was something to do with the sun, and something to do with Fenn. Perhaps, it was to do with God. The trunk of the tree was warm against her back. She stretched out her arm, and took hold of Fenn's hand. It was the first time, since she ceased to be a child, she'd touched another human being out of friendship.

## *Chapter Seventeen*

Two weeks later, May woke in the night. Why couldn't she sleep? May didn't know. Not something she'd eaten, she ate so little these days. Went off lunch by the time she cooked it. She hadn't done too much, but she'd taken some exercise; walked to the shops, and bought four ounces of pork pie. She really meant to finish the roses, but fell into a doze in the middle of the afternoon. They'd been wonderful this summer, the roses, going on so late. She couldn't help thinking as autumn came on, it might be her last season in this garden.

She climbed out of bed, testing her stiff knees speculatively. She might be spry when she got going, but it took some doing. She walked round the bedroom, clutching up handfuls of nightdress, so as not to trip over the hem. Not too bad. It must only be about midnight, she opened the curtains. Perhaps that was why she couldn't sleep. In the full moon, the garden was mysterious, silver, and drained of its own colours. It was also very still, although shadows of clouds passed across the moon, making the patches of light fade, the shadows reform.

She knew at that moment she wanted to walk in the moonlight. The need was insistent, it was irresistible. She smiled as she dressed. Growing old disgracefully, she thought, but not too sluttishly. She put on her brown lace ups, she would never be seen out of doors in her bedroom slippers. It's not disgraceful at all to need to walk in the moonlight. Once, a long time ago, she'd walked in the moonlight with Lewis.

It was warm, being still September, no need for a coat. Just her Shetland wool cardi. She walked quietly. Moving made the house creak, and Dodo would be asleep in the flat above. Quietly went through the door into the garden. On the path was a dead pigeon, the work, no doubt, of that dreadful cat, Vodka, or Mysterium, as Hughie insisted on calling it. Killing for the sake of it, then leaving the corpse for someone else to clear up. It looked as if it might have been sleeping peacefully, for it was quite unmarked. Fenn told her the cat was trying to create a pigeon-free zone.

May walked round the edge of the lawn, keeping the borders always on her left. In this way her walk seemed to be linear, as when they'd walked home from the Labour party hop, she and Lewis, on a night like this. They'd had to walk from one village to the next as they'd missed the last bus. On her left had been the life of the hedgerow, smelling of leaf mould and soggy grass, just as it did now. It seemed that then was now, and this garden was a long way in the past, less real than Lewis, even though he was not actually at her side.

He'd been wearing a green sports coat, rough to the touch. He'd held her hand, and pulled her along in time to his thinking, although she'd have preferred to walk slowly, and spin the time out for ever. He was excited by an argument he'd had about atheism.

It was when they saw the first lights of home that he'd stopped, and turned her round to face him. She remembered thinking how much she liked him, how he might lead her into a world she'd never known. She remembered how strong his face had looked, his teeth even and white in the landscape of his face, how certain he was of his destiny.

'How'd you like to marry a Labour Member of Parliament?' he said. Came out with it just like that. No preliminary words of love. That, when he hadn't even been selected to stand as a prospective member, let alone got into the House.

Her terrible mistake was in trying to save him. 'I couldn't possibly marry a Labour MP,' she said. 'I couldn't fit in with it.' So it was said, something she never meant to say, but her sharp tongue, really out of self-defence, came out with the words.

Of course she'd never meant she couldn't marry Lewis, just that she couldn't get on with the politics. She could still remember some of the people at that hop, they weren't her sort at all. They wouldn't have fitted in with the life she'd known in India. That was what she was really, what India had made her; more English than if she'd spent all her life in Oxford, or Richmond. No, she never meant she wouldn't marry Lewis.

But he thought she had. Nothing would change his mind about the Labour Party. He never got into Parliament, he stood where there were too many staunch Tories. May listened to the radio, married to dear Tom then, and heard he'd come second. Thank goodness there was only the wireless, she couldn't have borne to see his brave face on the television screen. Then he gave up trying, but she believed he wouldn't have changed the way he voted, not Lewis.

By the time they reached the village, he was silent, May quiet too. She would like to have said, ask me again, and I'll give you a proper answer. But she couldn't bring herself to say those words. It wouldn't have been correct. Girls must be asked. Not ever do the asking. He, having offered himself totally, wouldn't risk rejection again.

Soon after that evening walk, he moved away to work in Leeds. He wasn't a regular letter writer, and finally he stopped writing altogether. He just stopped loving her. He never gave her a second chance.

May walked the whole conversation over again in the moonlight, and was nearly home. She scrubbed her face dry with the back of her hand, and decided it was time to go inside, to come back home to the present. There were times when she could think about Lewis, and her thoughts would bring her comfort, but not tonight, not when it was so clear to her what she'd lost, and all through her own fault. Through her hasty tongue.

The door was locked, she'd shut it behind her without a second thought. It refused to open. She jiggled the handle hopefully, but nothing moved. She hadn't expected it not to open. Carefully she searched in her pockets, she couldn't have been stupid enough to come out without a key. It seemed she had. Neither had she slipped the latch up.

Upstairs Dodo's lights were all out. The same with Lex's flat above that. Some people would throw a pebble. I can't, thought May. Dodo would think I'm mad walking about in the moonlight. Lex probably wouldn't bother to get out of bed.

She decided to go for a proper walk, and went to the end of the road and back. Then she felt frightened, the world of night was peopled by strange and violent men. They were always in the papers. She would be attacked. By anyone. It would be over all the papers, with an unflattering photograph of her. She always took a poor photograph. She was also cold, very cold.

She had an idea. Perhaps Fenn or Hughie were still up. Either of them would understand what had happened. They wouldn't laugh. I'll take them a present, she thought. Fenn would make something tasty out of it. Pigeon was an underrated bird. It was almost as if their cat had thoughtfully left it for her to take round to them. She picked the bird up, and it was strangely comforting in its softness. She walked purposefully up the road, glancing about her, starting once as a night animal crackled the undergrowth in the hedge beside her.

But the windows of Fenn and Hughie's house were dark and unseeing. The Meadowcrofts would be sleeping peacefully. Sadly, she stared at the closed eyes of the house. The last thing she should do was wake them up. She'd ring the bell as soon as there were signs of life, nearer to morning. Gently, she lowered herself onto the door step, and prepared to wait.

When Fenn opened the front door next morning, she thought May was dead, frozen by the night, like a trapped sparrow. She looked much more frail than the substantial dead pigeon clutched in her arms.

## Chapter Eighteen

May warmed up to a faint pink and ate, with growing enthusiasm, a comforting bacon butty.

Hughie said gently, 'May, old thing, do you think the time's come for a bit of loving care?'

'No. Not yet.'

'If we'd been further into the winter, you could have died spending the night out in the cold. Hypothermia.'

'I won't do it again. I've learned my lesson.' May smiled pleadingly at Hughie before letting her head droop disconsolately to her shoulders.

'It might be something else next time. The gas stove. The bath. We want you to be safe, May.' Hughie took her hands and tried to make her look him in the eye, but she stared down at the fingers of her left hand, one now grown too slender for the wedding ring to stay firm.

May was stubborn. Hughie was firm. At last she cried and Hughie gave her a small brandy.

'I suppose you're right,' she whispered. Hughie held her like a lover until she grew calm. He telephoned Mellowstones then and there. They thought there might be a place as soon as ten days' time, and no more than a fortnight. Mrs Brown seemed to be on her way to another shore, distant but more serene. Mrs Lloyd Fermor needed to be moved downstairs, so Mrs Lomax could have the old day nursery, in many ways the most attractive room in the home. Mrs Lomax would enjoy the view.

The following Tuesday Matron phoned Hughie to tell him Mrs Brown had finally made it to the other shore, and they could go ahead with the arrangements for Mrs Lomax.

'We'll have a farewell dinner,' said Fenn. 'Make it special.'

She liquidized Stilton cheese and watercress for a paté, while Dodo burned the French toast, and Pru sat morosely at the kitchen table. 'He bought me coffee twice,' said Pru, 'and he was doing really well with his Russian. But that was it.'

'Think of his faults,' advised Dodo. 'The easiest way.'

'He kept his money in a purse. Put stuff on his hair. I suppose he looked a bit like Cecil Parkinson in his prime, around the top of his head.'

'Two coffees can't make up for that,' said Dodo firmly. 'You shouldn't have got your hopes up.'

'I'm unlucky. I sometimes think God's got it in for me.' Pru glanced towards her sister, hoping for a denial, even though Fenn had lapsed. Pru looked especially vulnerable, still in her candlewick dressing gown, clutching a mug of blackcurrant tea as if it were the thread of life.

'Pru, love,' said Fenn. 'Things change. Be patient, and just look forward to the dinner party tonight. We want everything to be lovely for May.' She put her arms round her sister, which was the least wise thing to do because it brought on the tears. Pru had cried a great deal since Fenn brought her home, but hopefully, that was therapeutic.

'Her last supper,' said Pru, and sobbed some more.

'Why don't you get a bath, and I'll make you some eggy breads. Food for solace.'

'Make that two,' said Dodo, who'd dropped by to check Lex was invited. 'Right. Pru, if the Doug's mums of this world can plot their own course, we can. You and me, Pru, are going to make things happen. I'm taking you in hand. We're going into town. This afternoon. You're to be transformed. How much can you afford?'

'Not anything really. I'm saving up.'

'What for exactly?'

'A cruise next autumn. The Ancient Greek Experience. A cultural tour with lectures in the evening, and English guides.'

'Then you certainly need to be shaped up for that. Listen to Dodo, and I'll guarantee you'll catch the Captain's eye.'

'I'm after culture, not sex.'

'Same thing with the Greeks. They were all at it. You've only got to look at the waiters today.'

'I don't know,' said Pru. 'Anyway, it's an English ship. There won't be any Greek waiters.'

'I'd better come with you,' said Fenn. 'Shopping, that is. We don't want anything taken to excess.'

'I may not,' said Dodo, 'be a success icon in the area of men, but I know a few truths where those sods are concerned. I shall pass them to you. My gift, Pru dear. Your future is about to blossom as you'd never have believed possible. Only trust me, Pru, and you shall walk on water.'

'I feel so tired,' said Pru, 'all the time.'

Dodo rejected all local, tried hairdressers, and selected one in the town by the appearance of the clientele as they emerged from the door. Ariadne was favoured by young, successful-looking women, but not the tarty. No ill-chosen rinses or startling highlights. On enquiry, the receptionist said there were no appointment times free for that afternoon.

'How disappointing for me,' said Dodo. 'Luckily my friend already has one for two o'clock.'

'Mrs Braint, is it?'

'Correct,' said Dodo, and pushed Pru forward, reckoning that once she got a wet head, it would be too late for them to turn her away.

'Dodo,' said Fenn, helplessly.

'We've hijacked someone else's time,' twittered Pru.

'Sssssh. You're OK so long as you insist you're Mrs Braint too,' whispered Dodo and shoved her towards the wash basins. They were all three relieved when Pru was shampooed beyond recall.

Dodo stood menacingly over Jeremy, the stylist, while he snipped and coaxed and pranced round Pru. He wore a cream satin shirt with gold cufflinks like conkers. His olive jeans fitted as snugly as the skin of an under-ripe apple. From time to time Dodo glanced appreciatively at his buttocks. She was aware, also, that there was a bit of a row going on at the reception desk behind them.

'Would madam care to sit down in reception?' suggested Jeremy.

'Certainly not. I'm keeping an eye on you,' said Dodo, and gestured him to keep cutting. Fenn sat on the stool upon which Jeremy sometimes alighted when he was cutting low.

'Give it line,' Dodo said. 'I want plenty of style. Shorter here, don't you think? We don't want a lot of weight over the eyebrows. Incidentally, Mrs Braint asked for you specially. She was recommended.'

'Delighted.' Jeremy fluttered his graceful eyelashes. 'May I enquire who by?'

'Name unknown,' said Dodo. 'She struck up a friendship on Concorde.'

'That would be Lady Snelsdon,' cooed Jeremy. 'She travels everywhere on Concorde. All the time. She's one of my most favourite clients.' He pronounced this as clee-awnt.

Pru closed her eyes and thought of Jesus on the cross as her familiar permed ends fell to the floor, and her nice, heavy, spectacularly level fringe became feathery and unreal.

Jeremy was an artist. Pru's hair became his challenge. He handled the drier like a juggler, throwing it from one hand to the other as he tackled Pru's head from every available approach, tweaking here, holding up a lock and letting it drift through his magical fingers as it blew in the warm breath of the drier, then a small hiss of styling mousse, a perfecting snip, a ruffle through, a firm tug, a tender pat. At last, Jeremy lifted up his hands as if offering a sacrifice of what was the very essence of beauty.

'I don't look like me,' said Pru nervously.

Jeremy made a final flourish with the spray, which he fired from the hip. He stood back, considering. 'I think your hair's lovely,' he said.

'Oh,' said Pru.

'Yes.'

Fenn stood beside her, smiling at her sister in the mirror. 'You've been discovered,' she said.

'Oh. Well, I must say,' agreed Pru, 'Jeremy certainly has done something.'

'I'll deal with paying,' whispered Dodo, and swept up to a suspicious receptionist. 'Wonderful. Jeremy has performed a miracle. I should have known Lady Snelsdon would only recommend the best.'

'We won't waste money on a facial,' decided Dodo. 'They can leave you looking blotchy. We'll get plenty of free advice when it's obvious you've come in to buy more than an eyebrow pencil.' In the event, it was mostly Dodo's advice that went into the choice of plum eyeshadow, mango lipstick, and double thickener chocolate mascara. 'You'll look good enough to eat.'

'Can we go home now?' said Pru. 'I can only stand so much on one day.'

It took a strong herbal tea and a slice of carrot and cinnamon cake at Natter's Tranquillity Tea House to stiffen her up. The pine furniture and waitresses in green gingham aprons were soothingly undemanding. 'You've got to get the right clothes,' said Dodo, 'if you're going to feel desirable.'

'We want something sexy that will make madam stand out,' said Dodo in Debenhams.

'We want something understated that will take madam anywhere,' said Fenn. The assistant was in twenties mode, with a long string of amber beads and holly-red lipstick. She didn't seem to understand either of them. Uncaringly, she held up polyester dresses with matching jackets, flock velvet blouses, skirts with elasticated waists.

'I don't really go anywhere,' whispered Pru, recoiling at the selections.

'You're going to a dinner party tonight for a start. May's last supper.'

'That's not out. Out, like a date.'

'It's a dinner date,' said Dodo firmly. 'Don't be negative. It's more than family. Lex will be there. He'll do anything for a cooked meal.'

'I don't like Lex.'

'Only because you used to be a little mouse and were frightened by him. You're not a mouse any more.'

Fenn went on her own search. 'Try this on.' She handed over a straight, burgundy skirt which came just above the ankle.

'I couldn't wear that. It's got a slit.' Pru touched the skirt nervously, 'though it's a lovely colour.'

'This, then,' said Dodo, proffering a clinging tube of red silk.

'Certainly not. It's what they wear in brothels.'

'Unlikely,' said Dodo, 'but you could try the skirt, at least.'

'Pure wool,' said Fenn, encouraging, and Dodo pushed Pru into a cubicle.

'At least it's got a slit,' said Dodo. 'We could slash it a bit higher, to show plenty of thigh.' They went in search of co-ordinated items. Pru nipped back out, and selected a turquoise taffeta dress, with a basque.

Fenn came back triumphantly, with a black camisole top, and soft, raspberry silk jacket. She had overcome Dodo's preference for the cerise revealing wrap-over blouse. They found Pru preening in the cubicle. 'Turquoise is my colour. Mummy always said so.'

'You look at the half-way stage between caterpillar and butterfly, all crisp and shiny. We're going for line and cut, Pru darling. This will make you feel slinky and sexy. It'll cling seductively. You'll positively hum when you're in it.'

'You can be very coarse, Dodo.'

'For your own good,' said Dodo, firmly hauling the taffeta dress off Pru. She helped her step into the skirt.

'It's not me.'

'Exactly. We're trying to make you not you. I'm looking at the new alluring Pru.'

'You don't think it's tarty, do you, the slit?'

'It's a sophisticated slit.'

Pru stared in the mirror, and Dodo sensed the wavering.

'Trust me. Now the silk jacket.' Dodo may not have been an expert at selecting clothes, but she could appreciate a stunning effect when she saw one.

Dodo realized the new Pru would make Dodo, herself, look older and fatter. Did that matter? Hughie was out of sight. Lex had no interest in her. She'd never got the measure of Lex.

'I think I'd feel happier in the turquoise,' dithered Pru.

With no sense of sacrifice at all, Dodo said, 'These clothes will make things happen. I know, and you don't, Pru. Be honest. Don't you feel more . . . dangerous?'

'I think I do.'

Fenn leaned against the mirror, her arms folded. She was tired of cooking, of supporting Hughie, of encouraging Pru, of worrying about Damaris. She looked at her sister, who seemed no longer the spinster, but a girl on the brink of her womanhood. For the first time she thought, I love my sister.

Pru wasn't merely someone to help, to battle for, to see as a responsibility. There was no need to shape, to guide. She needed only her space to grow, only Fenn's love, so that self-worth would let Pru flower. Dodo had given her space to grow by suggesting the spree in the first place. Fenn felt herself fall away, abandon her own power, her shaping energy. She smiled. 'How do you feel, with your hair looking like that?' she asked.

'Almost pretty?' Pru was rather shocked at her own lack of modesty. 'Well, Jeremy said I had nice hair.'

'He said it was lovely hair.'

'Yes, he did.'

'And it is.'

Pru inspected her hair again, using a hand mirror to see the back. She touched it, gently, with a sense of wonder. She looked at Fenn, and shook her head in disbelief.

'What are you going to do about that skirt?'

'Do you think I should have it?' It was scarcely a question, more a confirmation of the confidence she was beginning to realize.

167

'It's how you feel, Pru.'

Pru wondered, fleetingly, if she, Pru, were a bit attractive, after all. 'I think . . . Yes. I'll take them.'

'That's settled, then,' said Dodo. 'Now, you've got to show you feel sexy. Got to simmer. Relax the upper lip. Never clamp the jaws together. Lower the eyelids in a languid sort of way. Tits forward.'

Pru stretched up, tilted her head and let her eyelids drop by half a centimetre, while elongating the top lip. She didn't immediately achieve the required effect. Dodo stood beside her at the mirror, and demonstrated the languid eyelid technique.

The assistant put her head through the curtains. 'Is Modom feeling unwell at all?'

'Modom is doing her tension release exercises,' said Dodo. 'She suffers from executive stress. We'll take these three items, thank you.'

Lex brought Fenn five white roses. 'There are four extras, to disguise the single one,' he said quietly.

It took all the time needed to put them in a vase, and minutes more checking the table for Fenn's hand to stop shaking. By the time the meal was ready, she still wanted to hug him.

'A miracle,' said Hughie to Dodo, when Pru came into the dining-room with her drink, looking remote and mysterious, her silk jacket glowing softly in the low light.

'She was almost welded into a turquoise metallic come dancing outfit at one point,' said Dodo.

'It's wonderful of you all,' May said as she was seated first, the guest of honour. She liked the round table, it united the guests. There was a glass bowl in the centre in which floated five cinnamon-scented cream candles. Their tiny flames reflected in the polished mahogany beneath them. On a plate before her was a circle of

Stilton and watercress paté, set off by leaves of oakleaf lettuce.

May hoped they might say grace, but then she knew Hughie wouldn't think of that, and it was not usual these days except at weddings and functions. She momentarily closed her eyes and remembered what Jesus said at his last supper. She, too, would eat the bread and drink the wine in the knowledge of his love and the hope he would protect her at Mellowstones. She crumbled a little wholemeal roll on her side plate, Dodo's French toast never having come up to standard, then placed it paté-less, on the front of her tongue. On this occasion, she knew it didn't have to be blessed in order to remember HIM.

'You looked at your room today, May, I hear,' said Hughie.

'It's lovely,' said May, not letting on how unfriendly it seemed, despite every attempt to make it attractive. 'It's got a childish quality about it, as if it were still the day nursery. The bed's very small. It's new, of course, but in keeping. Cosy. They've kept the old black fireplace. I shall pretend that it's real coals, but it's artificial really. No-one would take coal up two flights of stairs today, would they?'

'It's a wonder anyone ever did,' agreed Hughie, peering suspiciously at the green specks in his paté.

Fenn watched her sister. Although Pru didn't speak much, it wasn't the silence of dullness, but of mystery. What was Pru thinking behind those downcast eyelids, touched with a hint of damson? 'You look fabulous,' whispered Fenn. 'Are you feeling great?' Pru gave an enigmatic smile. After all, Fenn wasn't to know the wired bra Dodo had insisted on buying was cutting into her left side something awful.

'Not long now before the girls come home,' said

Dodo. 'Did Damaris tell you they'd been to see that relative of yours in Adelaide, the one who's paralysed?'

'She said they went to the hospital, but that was all.'

'Marie said she was really upset. Wouldn't talk about it. Says Damaris hasn't been the same since. Very subdued.'

'Other people's pain has previously been outside Damaris's experience,' said Hughie.

Dodo sat between Lex and Pru. Lex seemed to have forgotten he'd met Pru before and leaned forward to talk across Dodo.

'What do you do, Pru?' Lex had already finished his paté and was keeping himself going with a third roll.

'Secretary. But I'm looking for a change of scene,' she said softly. 'I may even leave London.' To be near Fenn, to be near Dodo, who'd both been so lovely this afternoon, suddenly made the future bearable. She leaned forward to reply. Leaning forward seemed to get her away from the metalwork. She still felt weirdly unlike herself. The mirror in the bedroom had shown her a stranger, a woman who was no plainer than other women, a woman who had lovely hair. She remembered the caress of Jeremy's fingers as they worked.

She stayed leaning forward, looking at Lex, reluctant to get back into close contact with the underwiring. She couldn't remember exactly what had set her against Lex before. He was really rather nice. To be engaged in voluntary conversation was a novel experience.

'And you?' she asked, wide-eyed, as the wire caught up with her again.

'Teaching.' He didn't elaborate, as mocking St Anthony's would spoil May's treat.

'Tell me about working with Hughie, Lex,' said Dodo quietly, leaning slightly nearer to him. She wished she wasn't wearing her harlequin all-enveloping silk blouson top and slinky evening trousers. The latter were too tight, and the bright colours made her feel big. Already, she regretted her generous advice to Pru who was unaccustomedly smouldering, like a small provocative brazier in the snow.

Dodo put her elbow on the table, which helped to exclude Pru, and looked carefully at Lex, seeking for the last time that vital spark of interest.

Lex leaned back to talk to Pru behind Dodo's shoulder. 'How long are you staying here for?'

Dodo sighed and spread her paté thickly on her toast. She crunched noisily into it, spilling crumbs down her chin. There comes a time when food is the only reliable pleasure.

May realized the lamb was significant. Lamb had always been a biblical meal, an oblation, especially the sacrifice of the paschal lamb at the Jewish Passover. Unfortunately, the lamb came with rosemary, little spiteful sprigs of it, instead of mint sauce.

Lex, too, appreciated the sacrificial connotation. He'd have preferred goat, had there been a choice. In Holman Hunt's *Scapegoat*, he recognized his own lot. Whatever had made him apply for that job in New Zealand? He didn't want to go to New Zealand, any more than May wanted to go to Mellowstones.

When Dodo went to the loo, before the chocolate and grape gateau appeared, Lex moved into her seat, next to Pru. He moved the glasses and napkins, making it clear that he wouldn't be swopping back again.

Fenn watched her dinner party, this coming together that she'd created, this communion of souls. Fenn sensed the dance of fortunes that formed a pattern, a pattern not fixed and finite, but one of change, like music ever developing, never repeating except in a different form. The dance was at her table, a fellowship of people as they touched briefly, in the motif of their lives, yet to move on. She no longer wanted to pin down the pattern, catch the butterfly wings, she was not, now, the orchestrator. Instead, she listened to the harmony, to Dodo's low notes on the cello, to the theme of a single white rose, to May in a sad minor key. There were other cadences she didn't quite catch. Perhaps the dance was about to change once more, perhaps there was nothing she could do about it. It was good to see Lex chatting up Pru, it was what she needed.

Fenn thought of the rose, the single white rose, and its attendants, which hid the secret that Lex had given her a mark of love, instead of a polite gift from a guest.

'More pud, Dodo?' As she served, she looked up, and smiled at Lex.

'Absolute heaven,' said Dodo. From now on, she resolved to dedicate herself to the pleasures of the palate. Such happiness was always available.

Later, May surprised herself by not crying herself to sleep. Instead, she stared out of the window at the garden in its darkness, waiting for what was to come. The Japanese anemones gleamed ghostlike and white in the darkness, the sedums, being pink, were less reflective. The Garden of Gethsemane, too, must have been very beautiful. It was spring then, of course.

## Chapter Nineteen

Fenn and Hughie took May to Mellowstones at tea time. When they left, Sister Birch took over and brought sandwiches and a pot of tea to her room. 'You probably want to settle in,' she said, 'arrange your belongings.' Her fat, high-coloured face was mildly sympathetic. 'There's a box of tissues on the window-sill. We'll see you at dinner. That's at seven. If you like, you can find me in the kitchen, and I'll introduce you to our other guests.'

'Thank you,' said May bravely. Alone, she looked round the room, which would now always be her home, she would know no other, unless it were to be a hospital bed. She pottered about, unpacking the books she'd brought, hanging her clothes in the wardrobe, which seemed far too big for what she had. She wondered if one were expected to wear different clothes every day. The toy cupboard was painted inside, and extra shelves fitted. There was no sign of the rocking horse.

She sat in her own rattan chair, delivered earlier, and wrote to Hughie to thank him for all he'd done. Then she waited for seven o'clock, and felt sick inside.

Dinner was comfortingly unmodern, with packet soup, chicken casserole with cabbage, and a soothing rice pudding with tinned apricots. May ate little. She sat at a table with two other women and a man. One woman

173

was far too busy getting the better of her false teeth to speak at all. She did, however, gaze at May from under her lavender-rinsed sausage curls, showing disdain for May's own no-nonsense straight hair pulled back into a bun. May was relieved not to be with Duncan, Molly or Doris, whom she'd seen at the sale preview.

Norman told her about his wife, who had died three years ago, and their plans to retire to Hunstanton. The second woman was called Pearl.

'What do you think of this place then?' Pearl demanded. 'I've only bin here three weeks meself.'

'It seems very pleasant.'

'Bleeding boring, I say. Hard to tell it from a morgue. Norman here's been raised from the dead, haven't you, Norman?'

He nodded appreciatively. 'They thought I was gone,' he said. 'Couldn't find a pulse. Wasn't breathing. And me dreaming I was going down a great white path. Then Sister Birch comes down on my chest like Frank Bruno, they tell me, and I'm back in the land of the living.'

'If you say so,' said Pearl.

The other woman finally overcame her dentures. 'I'm afraid I don't find you a peaceful influence in this home, Pearl. I shall ask Sister Birch to see that we don't sit together in future. Now if you'll excuse me, I must organize my bridge table for this evening.' She wobbled over to the door.

'Bleeding snob,' said Pearl. 'Want me to show you the telly room? Nothing decent on, of course, until after the kids have gone to bed.'

'Actually, I have a few things to do,' said May. 'Must get myself straight, you know.'

In the safety of her room May did cry, though she'd held out longer than Sister Birch would have expected. At nine-thirty a West Indian nurse, very young and pretty, brought her a mug of cocoa. She wasn't too young to tactfully ignore the tears. 'Or there's tea, if you prefer,' she said. 'I can easily get it.'

'Cocoa's fine, thank you.' May kept her face turned away, and was grateful the girl didn't linger.

When the tears stopped, May wondered if, like the other bodily juices, they became less prolific with age. She didn't feel tired enough yet to sleep. In fact, she felt strangely clear-headed. She drew back the curtain and looked down into the garden. She tried to imagine it as she'd seen it from the day nursery before. There were sculptured hedges, and the light caught the odd last rose. Otherwise, the night was black and desperately sad. Here, at last, her journey was virtually over, the tram had passed its penultimate stop.

She was here because she made mistakes. She was cold and buttoned up, so tied to what was what, so unspontaneous. It was her fault Lewis had gone. Perhaps it was her fault Rose had gone too, her fault that she hadn't had more babies. She'd not been a bounteous, fruitful, milk-laden woman, but prim and flat-chested and measured with her love. She closed the curtains and looked round the room. She was lucky to be here. She kneeled beside the bed after she turned the cover down.

God didn't exactly speak to her, she didn't have a relatable experience, to be passed on as proof of his existence, but she recognized his will within her heart, as is the way with those who have lived long in the knowledge of his love.

She recognized she must serve him in these last months, or perhaps years, heaven forbid, that were left to her. She must live in the real world. She must forgo the comfort of imagining little Rose when she was trying to sleep, she'd stop creating the world as it was not. Instead, she'd bring the grace of God to this home. She'd integrate Pearl with those who'd been born into

175

the middle classes. Pearl would be God's work. She'd never stop trying to help Fenn to regain her faith. As she went to sleep, she wondered why the one thing for which she never prayed was to see Lewis again. Perhaps because she knew that could never happen.

In the morning, May walked in the garden. She found a white painted garden seat situated so one could look back at the house through an avenue of rose arches. The house was early Victorian. It would once have sheltered a single family, with many laughing children and maids who worked all hours. It was almost all gone now, that way of life. Perhaps May's life had gone full circle, from the privileged life in India to now, living in the large house once again. But no, it wasn't full circle. It was completely changed. Life wasn't as it had been before. Wrong paths had been taken. Life had not worked out. She had no child to visit her in this place.

'Bleeding cold,' said Pearl, coming up behind.

'You're fond of the garden too?' May moved up on the bench. At least Pearl was neither a bore, nor a snob.

'Not me, never. It's the only place I can go for a fag. It's OK in the conservatory, but it's being cleaned and they won't let me in. Have one yourself.'

'No thanks. I've never smoked.'

'Get black looks in the conservatory, I can tell you. Those bridge snobs are trying to get Sister Birch to stop that and all. You got to have a few healthy vices, I say, otherwise you might as well be dead.' Pearl was rolling her own, and very deft she was. 'Go on. Try it. Prove you're not one of them blue tops.'

May drew back her shoulders and thought of Norman sinking into his living death. She thought of Lewis who would never grow old. She thought of the narrowness of her life, and all the things she hadn't done. Being

176

buttoned up, and correct and good had brought her nothing in the way of happiness.

'I might just try one,' she said. 'Just one. Why not?'

They sat together in the last sunshine of the autumn. May thought, two old ducks, who'd never come together in the normal way of things. She began to feel extraordinarily mellow, almost as if it were summer. She felt generous and contented. 'If you like,' she said, 'I could teach you to play bridge, and we could join the snobs. Though why you think bridge snobbish, I can't imagine.' Of course it wasn't snobbish. Every one is equal. I wish Lewis were here now. 'I played a lot in India. We all did. It was fairly boring really.'

'I don't like curry,' said Pearl. May was probably an old snob as well, but she was talking to her, Pearl, as if they were equal. Proves I'm as good as them, any day, she thought.

'Do we get coffee at about now?' asked May.

'Soon. Here, have a nip if you're cold.' Pearl produced a bottle of rum from her handbag. 'Don't let them see from the house. Sister keeps nicking my supply. She must have a distillery by now.'

'Why not?' said May and took a good swig. 'I really don't know what's come over me. That cigarette's made me quite abandoned.'

'It's great stuff,' said Pearl. 'You'd think they'd legalize it, wouldn't you?'

'How are we doing . . . er, May?' The Vicar felt the use of her Christian name might be more comforting in the circumstances, help her to see him as a friend. He dropped into a chair, leaning forward, elbows on his outspread knees, fingers interlaced below the chin.

'Quite well, thank you, Vicar. Everyone seems very pleasant.'

177

'It's so easy to lose faith, at times like this. I know that.'

'Everything . . .'

'I do understand God can seem hopelessly remote, that he's never there when you need him.'

'William . . .'

'I have to confess to you, May, I feel like that myself, sometimes. You see, you're not alone.' He moved his chin from his hands, and put his forehead on them instead. For a moment, May wondered if he were praying. Then he looked up. 'Nothing is easy, May.'

'I'm so sorry, William. Whatever's happened to you?' She hoped it wasn't something indiscreet, in a public loo.

'May, who am I to comfort you? Why doesn't God save his church? You're another one gone. Soon, they'll all have left. Fenn, she went for no good reason. I go through the words, and no-one listens. The flower guild bickers, the choirboys threaten to go on strike. I've got to go on. I have to provide for the family.' He bent his head forward, the blond hair falling down across his face. 'Soon, it will all have gone. It seemed so safe, choosing the church.'

Slowly, very gently, May leaned forwards and took his hands in her own. 'You'll come through it, William, I'm sure you will. Stop praying, and listen instead. I've met emptiness, but not any more. Really, William, I've come through. So will you.'

He looked up, and his denim-blue eyes were wet. Then he smiled. 'Of course I will. Of course. You're a wonderful woman, May. I came here to cheer you up.'

'You have done, William. Yes, you have. Really.' She let go of his hands and sat back. At last, after all these years, God was using her. She, May, was a conduit for God's will to those on this earth, and, this morning, to William, of all people.

*     *     *

'It's called a throw,' said Fenn, 'because you throw it over things.'

'You've given me so much,' said Pru, and was prepared to get tearful, but tossing the Indian blanket over the sofa, trying to get a casual effect, proved to be therapeutic.

'You'd never think this was May's place, even though you're buying some of her furniture.' They'd spent all day moving Pru in.

'It's my place,' said Pru, and sat on the sofa, hugging her knees to her. 'Would you like some tea?'

'Lovely.'

Fenn tried not to look out of the window at the path which led to the communal front door. Hughie would be home by now, so Lex might walk in any moment.

She hadn't seen him since May's supper party when he gave her flowers. She was tempted to keep one white rose and press it under the sitting room carpet. But she resisted. When they faded, Fenn put the roses on the compost heap, not in the dustbin.

In the kitchen Pru put cups on a tray. She felt at home already. Of course, there was Dodo upstairs, warm, funny Dodo. There was even Lex, a man who could pop in to change a plug for her. Come to think of it, she wasn't at all certain Lex would be able to change a plug.

She took a packet of digestives into the sitting-room. Fenn was looking pensive, staring at the front fence. Pru put her arms round her sister. She was surprised how huggy she'd become recently.

'Mrs Lomax is having a busy morning,' said Sister Birch, brisk and in control. 'She's helping Pearl to fit in. We're quite surprised at that little friendship, but there you are. It takes all sorts.'

She led Fenn along the hall, through the sitting-room

179

and to the conservatory, which was earthily muggy with the smell of damp soil and hot water piping. To meet May in a public room must be an improvement. On each of Fenn's two previous visits, May had taken her up to the privacy of her bedroom, making tea with her electric kettle. Even her stoical insistence that she was very happy at Mellowstones couldn't disguise her inner bewilderment. As she sat perched on the bed, insisting Fenn had the only chair, she looked smaller, and frail, as if she could be crumpled up like a ball of paper.

Now, May sat at one side of a bamboo table. Opposite was a woman wearing an ochre polyester dress encrusted with purple plastic bugle beads. Her hair was shoulder-length with curly ends, a style much-favoured just after World War Two. Between them, playing cards lay face up on each edge of the table. May was smoking a cigar.

'Come and join us, Fenn, I'm teaching Pearl to play bridge. Going through the bidding. She's coming along very well. You do know Pearl, don't you? She's Doug's mother. Fancy that. I've only just discovered myself.'

'I know Doug,' said Fenn, shaking hands.

'And I'm teaching May what she's missing, aren't I duck?' said Pearl, smiling coyly out from her sheep-coloured locks. 'She's not that slow at finding out what's a comfort in life.'

'Smoking, and er . . . that sort of thing?' asked Fenn warily.

'What does she mean by that, me old flower?' cooed Pearl.

'I know exactly what she means,' said May. 'Don't worry, Fenn. We've renounced the cannabis, haven't we, dear?'

'Only because Doug got raided by Sister, so supplies have dried up. I do miss me little puff now and again. Sweetens 'ard feelings.'

Fenn decided Pearl didn't seem nearly as evil as Doug made her out to be.

'Found me place in the sunshine. And now I've got May as me mate. Treats me like a nob. We have a good larf, don't we, flower?'

'Of course we do, Pearl. Many a good laugh together. Now I think I'll take a little stroll round the garden with Fenn before it gets dark. If I were to bid three spades, you can be working out what you'd respond.'

'We'll go for game, May. Always go for game, whatever the odds.' Pearl swapped her two of diamonds for the ace out of the opponents' cards.

'You could make us a pot of tea. We could have it together,' suggested May.

'Three teabags or four?' asked Pearl, pleased she was still counted in.

'Proper tea, dear, not teabags,' said May. 'I have some Earl Grey in the cupboard.'

Pearl preened, and winked conspiratorially at Fenn.


Already the tips of daffodil leaves had thrust themselves optimistically to the light, a hint of hope in the dying garden. The faded rose-coloured sedums were tarnished with mildew, and their once succulent leaves hung yellow and rubbery like the spent teats of babies' bottles. The late chrysanthemums were burned by frost, the leaves black and slimy. As ever, Christmas roses nestled, curled up within their stems, reluctant to show for their name day. Fenn and May walked slowly along the path which led between lawn and border.

'Sometimes, I think winter is the least dead of the seasons,' said Fenn. 'The flowers may be out of sight, but really, the whole year is coiled up in a sort of potential, just waiting to be. Perhaps it's reached Nirvana, achieved perfect equilibrium.'

'Sounds a funny idea to me.'

'Hughie thinks it's funny, too. There are so many things I can't explain to him. He only wants to know nothing changes.'

'Hughie's a lovely man.'

'I know that May. It's just . . . Let's get back to you. Pearl seems quite a character.'

At the end of the path was a seat, one of the many in the Mellowstones' grounds. May dusted it with a paper handkerchief from her pocket. 'Free issue.' They sat down. 'I've come to think there's no such thing as happiness and unhappiness,' she said, 'only acceptance.'

'That sounds rather bleak.'

'Accepting God's will. The mistake is not to recognize it. I'm content now, I'm on my own. I don't have to fret about what will happen to me. I don't fret about what might have been different. I can live in the present.'

Fenn put out her hand and covered May's cold fingers. 'You mean you can accept losing the baby? Rose?'

'Yes, and other things. There are things I feel I could do. Like marry a man who voted Labour.'

'Oh,' said Fenn. 'I always thought Tom was the only one for you.'

'Lewis was before Tom. I never thought I'd talk about him. Now, it doesn't matter. You'd have liked Lewis. He trod his own path. I often wonder . . .' She swallowed. 'Pearl is fun. She makes me see a different side of myself. Incidentally, I shopped Doug to Sister. Don't ever let on, will you? Cigars are one thing, only smart young things smoked them when I was a girl. But cannabis. Well, I'm still a bit of a snob, I suppose. How's everything with you?'

'Pru's settling into your flat. Hughie has a complete list of what she'd like to buy. Then he'll check with you about selling the rest.'

'He's so good to me. I'm glad Pru will be there, not some stranger. Is she feeling happier?'

'Much more settled. She's hoping for a post at St Anthony's.'

'I wonder how Lex is? Dodo said he might come and see me. He's been on a course for two weeks, she said.'

'A course? Really? How wonderful.' Fenn almost laughed. That was why she hadn't seen him.

'I don't think it's a specially wonderful course,' said May.

'Perhaps he and Pru will become friends,' said Fenn, lightly.

'I thought it might be you he liked,' said May, her eyes very button-like and bright. 'I notice things, you know.'

'What a funny thing to say.'

'I wouldn't have mentioned it, once. But now that it's nearly all over for me, I wish I didn't have so many regrets. I can accept them now, but there have been so many. Hughie, of course, is very like Tom. He was all I had.'

'You're not suggesting I have a fling, are you?'

'I hope you don't have regrets, that's all. We'd better get back for the Earl Grey. I don't want Pearl putting rum in it.'


The Earl Grey was thick and stewed, and not enhanced by full cream milk.

'Did you know Damaris and Marie come home next week? Via India. They're flying in from Delhi next Wednesday.'

'It'll be good to see Damaris again.' May wanted to say, like Rose coming to see her, but managed not to.

'Are men allowed in here?' Lex stood in the doorway, looking neither arrogant nor cynical, but smart, and smaller, in a tie and a blazer. He sat uncomfortably on his wicker chair and ate the small fish paste sandwiches Sister Birch brought to them.

'You do look nice,' said May, noticing the tie.

'I didn't want to let you down,' said Lex. 'Especially as I may not see you again before Christmas. We're always frantic at the end of this term, concerts and things, you know. We're doing a post-modernist sketch of the Christmas story. My philosophy group wrote it. Sorry. Shouldn't have mentioned that. I've brought you a pressie.' He handed her a small parcel wrapped untidily in Christmas paper.

'A present. How very exciting. I haven't got to wait until Christmas, have I?' May was already tearing at the paper. It was a brief edition of the Book of Kells, bound in holly-green cloth. He'd bought it out of a charity Christmas catalogue addressed to the previous occupant of the flat. He'd loved the Celtic illuminations, felt interested in the Pagan influences on the new Christianity when it first came to Britain. It wouldn't be quite the present May thought it was. It might make her think.

'Lex. What a surprise. Fancy you choosing this for me. It's so beautiful.'

'That's class for you,' said Pearl. 'I think I'll ask my Doug to get me one. He'll know where there's a lorry one'll have fallen off of.'

'With you not believing . . . it's generous, Lex.' May began to worry how she could organize a present in return.

'I rather like the fiction of a megalomaniac who had things fall lucky in the end,' said Lex. 'Hell. I'm sorry. I really didn't mean to be like this.'

May surprised herself by laughing, and wondered whether Pearl had slipped something into the tea after all. 'You know, you remind me very much of someone I once knew, of whom I was very fond. Very fond indeed.'

'I knew it,' said Lex. 'You've got a murky past.'

'It wasn't murky in the least, unfortunately,' said May. 'He was an arguer, just like you. His name was Lewis.'

'My Granpy's called Lewis. My mother's father,' said Lex.

'Lewis Kingdom.' May closed her eyes for a moment. Today was the first time she'd spoken to anyone of him since she'd married Tom, and she'd done it twice.

'I don't believe it.' Lex put his sandwich down.

'What's that outside the window?' said Fenn suddenly. 'It's a man skulking in the shrubbery.'

'It's my Doug,' cried Pearl, standing up and waving to him. 'He's avoiding that Sister Birch. I wonder if he's got any fresh supplies.'

Doug sidled in through the garden door. 'That woman's not here, is she?' He tiptoed to the door into the house and looked round it warily. 'Dracula's wife.'

'She's a very nice lady,' said Pearl. 'It's only you brings out her fascist tendencies. You know my friend Mrs Lomax?' She pulled May slightly forward to show propriety. 'What have you brought?'

'A small bottle of sweet sherry. That'll have to do you. The old bag threatened you'd be expelled if she found any of the other again. And no spirits either. It's your age.'

'Share with others, that's what I always say,' said Pearl, and slopped a generous drop of sweet sherry into all the half empty cups, 'in the hope that they'll share with you back. Specially when most people have got a lot more than what I've got.'

'You enjoying yourself in here, then, are you?' asked Doug, anxious doubt in his voice.

'Now I've got me mate,' said Pearl. 'And I'll know I've arrived when old snobby blue-top asks me to make up at cards.'

'Bridge,' said May. 'You must call it bridge, dear, not cards. You're doing very well, I must say.'

'What are you looking so miserable about?' Pearl asked. 'We're having a lovely high-class social, and you come in looking like you've lost your libido.'

'Nothing's wrong with me.' Doug looked round at the company, and smiled fiercely. It wasn't how he'd planned it at all. Fenn Meadowcroft was sitting there, looking as if she owned the place. Ma looked chipper. May Lomax shouldn't have been looking more relaxed than he'd ever seen her, but with strangely elated eyes, wide, no longer small and button-like. She was smiling at that oddball Lex as if he were a football pool she'd won.

How could his well-plotted revenge on the middle classes have turned out so happily?

'Anyway,' said Pearl, 'Mrs Lomax is going to pray for you.'

## Chapter Twenty

Fenn bought some fresh tuna from Corrigan's. Corrigan thought Mrs Meadowcroft had changed. It wasn't her cameo bones that struck him first these days, or her chirpy nose, it was her eyes. They were dreamy, with a smile in them. She wore no make-up, but the lids, rather heavy, were lightly veined with mauve. She used to be brisk, summing up each piece of fish on his slab, discerning the best buy. This morning she floated in, wearing a black coarse-knit cape, and said, 'Oh, tuna. I think I'll have some tuna.' Not a bit like she used to be. Her hair was different, too. It was always needing restraint, in knots and bands and buns. Now it hung free, in a long bob, shining like wet seaweed.

He wasn't to know she was cross with Hughie, who was threatening to ban Lex's post-modernist Christmas play at school.

'It's all about doubts,' said Hughie. 'Mary doesn't know who the father of the child is.'

'Sounds contemporary,' said Fenn. 'It was a lot to swallow.'

'We can't have that, you know. We're C of E at St Anthony's.'

'You're being childish.'

As Fenn came out of the fish shop, discomforted by Corrigan's stare, she saw Lex emerge from the post office. He licked some stamps and put a brown envelope into the letter box. 'My manuscript off to another lucky publisher,' he said. 'I fancy some coffee. Come and have one too. You'll have the pleasure of talking to me on neutral ground.'

The smell from The Pot Pourri Coffee Place was enticing, though Fenn never went in there herself. She thought of the white rose, and she thought of May's regrets. She thought of Hughie and the C of E.

'Why not?' she said. Coffee and adultery were miles apart.

'So the book's finished then? Pleased with it? I thought you said it'd already gone off somewhere.'

'Picked a house where they were a bit thick. Yes, I am pretty pleased with it, now. Got it polished.'

Fenn warmed her fingers round her coffee cup and looked at Lex across the brim. 'Perhaps you'll be famous.'

'Probably.' He gave her the full treatment, of smiling with his eyes only. He'd worked that one out in the bathroom mirror.

'I hear Woodhouse has had his medication stepped up again. It seems he mightn't be back. I'm trying hard not to upset Hughie at school, by the way. I'm sticking to the syllabus like chewing gum on a shoe.'

Fenn looked back at him and found herself smiling, as she did when she first bumped into him. It was his sense of fun, sense of the ridiculous, that was so infectious, that could surprise her, could make her laugh.

'There are other things on my mind, actually.'

'Yes?' Fenn looked down into her coffee. She never thought she'd allow him the chance to say what she thought he was going to say. Briefly, she wondered if she'd got it wrong, and he was going to tell her he fancied the new Pru.

'I've been offered another job. Heard this morning.'

'Exciting,' said Fenn. 'Promotion?'

'Head of department. There's one small snag.'

'Yes?'

'It's in New Zealand.'

'Well away from the limitations of English values?' She was careful not to let him see she was jolted.

'English values is what they're asking for, actually.'

'I hope you find them more receptive than St Anthony's.'

'Experimental school. Teaching through logic. It's because I've written about exactly that that they offered it to me. I had the briefest interview, last week, with some bloke of theirs in London. I managed to give the impression that publishers were still fighting it out to get the contract.'

'Are you going to take it?' Part of her was relieved she was wrong, his attention to her hadn't been a joke, mere teasing. Somewhere else, she felt a pleasure was torn away from her.

'It depends, I suppose.'

'On what?'

'On what I decide.'

Fenn looked down and saw her own neat fingers, her rings, and beyond them, her basket on the floor, with its fish for lunch, and a wholemeal loaf. Her life was so safe, so easy. But Lex had a frayed shirt cuff, his hair needed a wash, his oversized coat was getting bobbles of fuzz round the elbows, and he didn't know on which side of the world he wanted to live.

She felt generosity within her, wanting to comfort him, to care for him, wanting him to be happy too. She wasn't prompted by her own need. Putting the coffee cup down, she leaned closer, across the table.

'Lex,' said Fenn. 'Lex.' She wanted to hug him. 'Might you be lonely?' She'd forgotten about the rose. It was the mother in her who spoke. She saw he'd not

189

shaved that morning. Her eyes felt the roughness of his skin.

'Not if you come with me.' He put his hands over hers.

Doug sauntered down the street. He fancied a coffee. He checked through the window that the caff wasn't full. Didn't want to look a fool having to walk out because there was no empty table. 'Well, up yours,' he said.

Forget the coffee. There was a real chance to even scores. Fancy that snooty Fenn Meadowcroft holding hands with the arty fellow from the flat on top of Dodo's. He turned and briskly walked back to Springfield Lane. This was one for Hughie Meadowcroft, and all his bloody private school stood for. Doug had made certain assumptions about St Anthony's results and the burning shame over Murray's failure with A-levels was still to be quenched.

Fenn tried to pull her hand away, but Lex wouldn't let go. 'Don't say things to embarrass me,' she said.

'Can't help it. You're so funny when you get flustered.'

His hand felt warm and rough-skinned. He moved his thumb to and fro across the backs of her fingers. She wondered how such a little movement could feel so loving. And so disconcerting. With more determination, she pulled her hand away.

'Hughie's going to a seminar next Monday, you know. Away all day,' said Lex.

'I know. He's been preparing notes. God help any post-modernist who tries to argue the text is created by the reader.' Damn Hughie, he was in a state about his lecture, and he was going to be just as stupid about the school play.

190

'Hughie's little foible. Let's have lunch while he's away. Or are you going to get in a tizz about that as well?'

'I don't get in a tizz about anything.'

'So you will, then?'

'All right.' For goodness sake, lunch was only lunch, she thought.

'All right? You actually said "All right"?'

'I believe I did.'

'Before you change your mind, let's say your place. I'll be round about twelve forty-five.' Before she could protest, he stood up, brushed the top of her head lightly with his mouth, and walked out. Fenn had to pay for the coffee.

She walked back slowly. Why had she agreed to lunch at home? It was not the same as lunch out. Not at all. The very words, 'your place' had connotations. It was not a term available in her youth, but people said 'my place' or 'your place' all the time on the telly when . . .

She thought what May'd said about regrets. She felt, sometimes, she could hit Hughie for his predictability. It was as if he were hanging onto her feet when she was trying to swim. Anyway, nothing more had to happen than lunch, and Lex was going to New Zealand. Probably going to New Zealand.

She felt the top of her head where he'd touched her lightly as a moth's wing, and was amazed that it felt quite as normal.


'I've come for me dusters.' Doug stood on the door step, threateningly near to the door when Hughie opened it. He was dressed casual. Instead of his tartan wool shirt, he seemed only to have a vest on under his dayglow orange anorak.

'Mrs Meadowcroft is not in, I'm afraid.'

'Your dusters is,' said Doug. 'I thought they could do with a wash.' He looked at Hughie. What a pervert, he was wearing a tie on a Saturday. How unctuous he looked, how smug. Just because he worked in a poxy private school, teaching idiots whose parents bought them university places with money, he thought he was above everyone. How would those kids have done going to the comp, where they didn't coach you for the special entrance to Oxford, but you had to take your luck in the A-level shambles? He needed teaching a lesson himself, that's for sure. Kids from poxy schools keeping real talent out. That's what he was about.

'That's very good of you,' said Hughie. 'How considerate.'

'Vroom is an ace service.' Doug pushed past and went to the kitchen. Hughie followed him casually. He'd never considered Doug to be completely above suspicion, and it seemed strange to come round on Saturday morning only to collect some dusters to wash.

'I knew Mrs Meadowcroft wasn't home,' Doug went on, 'but I thought you would be.'

'You seem to know a great deal. Mrs Meadowcroft is usually home at this time.'

'Can't be in two places at once, can she?'

'Not usually, no.'

'It was when I saw her in the caff that I was reminded of the dusters you see.'

'In the caff?' asked Hughie, as Doug had intended.

'That posh place, the Po purry.'

'Pot Pourri.'

'Yes there. Having a nice cup of coffee and an interesting conversation, by the look of it.'

'We usually have coffee together on a Saturday. Here. Was she with Dodo?'

'She wasn't with a lady.' Doug picked up his dusters and made certain to catch the expression on Hughie's face. He marched to the door and was wrong in believing that Hughie would ask another question. He was forced, therefore, to abandon being the innocent giver of truthful answers, to become the informer. 'It was him from the flat at the top of Mrs Lomax's, if you want to know. He appeared to be holding Mrs Meadowcroft's hand. In all innocence, I'm sure. She's such an attractive lady, I've always said. They were far too engrossed to notice me, I'm afraid.'

'Everyone loves to talk to my wife,' said Hughie with dignity. 'She has time for everyone. Even people like that.'

'Quite,' said Doug, and took himself off with an obsequious smirk.

Hughie sat in the study, in the middle of the sofa, and sank his shoulders. The cleaner was a disgusting man, permanently on the brink of belching. That a story of Fenn having coffee with the charlatan Lex, should come from him made the news all the more unpalatable. Such a slimy method, full of unspoken innuendo. He must have made it up about holding hands.

How could Fenn have coffee with a man that she knew her husband so disliked? He'd never have thought Fenn would do that. Of course, there'd be nothing wrong in it, nothing personal, he trusted her totally. But temptation could come. He knew that. He winced at the memory of Dodo gazing up into his face with hints of delights.

He could see Doug's evil face, smiling, imagining whole areas of misconduct and intrigue. Of course he trusted her.

He felt he was in a boat which had something wrong with the steering. Fenn guided his life, she kept him safe. Fenn soothed him, she knew his needs, she was the only one who understood how insecure he really was. But now Fenn was steering the boat like a mad thing, drinking coffee in a public place with the enemy. If only that was all it was.

Did she know what she meant to him? She must do. He didn't have to tell her. She knew. He never needed to tell her. He had told her, a long time ago, and so she knew. He looked round the comforting brown walls of the study, his own retreat to the womb, his sanctuary. He gazed at the books, the brown curtains, at the dun-coloured sofa covers, and the window frames painted to resemble oak. Thus it had always been. Slowly, like water climbing a flower stem, he knew Fenn didn't love this room as he did.

## Chapter Twenty-One

Hughie watched Fenn collect the cartons of plates to put in the boot. He said nothing about Doug's visit, but yesterday he watched her, seeking a sign that Fenn, unchangeable Fenn, was different. He saw nothing. She was different about this church nonsense, of course, and he was only just getting used to her hair, but Fenn never really changed, as his wife, that was. She always looked after him, he always was safe with her.

'Are you sure you don't mind me working on a Sunday? I'm sorry. I should have turned it down.'

'Nothing you can do now.' He drank his coffee, and decided that, still, she looked no different.

'It's further afield, you see. I was flattered to be asked to go thirty miles to cook.'

'I'll get tea for when you get back.'

'I'll be late. I'll wash up there, if I can. Could you carry these boxes for me?'

'Take all the time you need,' said Hughie. The longer the better, he added to himself.

He watched her drive away and rinsed his coffee cup.

Even as he'd sat in the study the previous morning, on Doug's departure, he'd realized what he must do. He'd taken her for granted. He'd always taken her for granted. Once he declared his love, it became a fact.

It was. It existed. Talking about it wasn't necessary. He wasn't a man who changed.

But Fenn changed, subtly, gradually, so he hardly noticed it happening. She wasn't so efficient, for a start. She didn't go on all day about how stupid Dodo was. She looked different too. Wore things that flowed all over the place, wafted about. All rather nice, and he liked her hair short and loose, whatever he'd thought to the contrary. But there was all this stupid meditation, sitting under trees with her eyes closed, or breathing in a special way while she was supposed to be eating her toast.

Hughie knew he must act. He depended too much on her, he might be the provider, but she was the giver. She made his life everything that it was. Without her, his life could not be. But he could see Fenn going on just the same, if he weren't around, getting a bit loopier perhaps.

He didn't believe what Doug had told him. It simply couldn't be true, but it served as a little reminder. The time had come to act, to do something that would really please her. He put on his anorak, and strode down the road.

The wedding anniversary lunch went well. Admittedly, an alcoholic great aunt tripped over the Alsatian and broke her fibula. A grandchild unfortunately heaved a potted begonia through the patio doors in a paddy, but the food was superb. The salmon melted. The salad was perky. The hot winter fruits were a surprise. The brandy ice cream held up. People asked for her business card. Fenn drove home happily, feeling ready for the cup of tea Hughie'd promised.

The smell, as she opened the front door, prepared her, but not totally.

The hall was piled high with books. They were on

the stair treads to each side, leaving a narrow channel for emergency trips to the loo. Books which could not be accommodated in the hall, or on the stairs, were in the dining-room, high on the table, and on the floor, concealing the window.

Hughie came out of the study. He wore his out-worn striped pyjamas which had been put in the rags drawer to become polishers. He waved a brush loaded with paint, pale Buttermilk. 'You do like the colour?' His expression was that of a child, bringing home his first hand-made Easter card.

'Hughie. Hughie, it's wonderful. It's beautiful. But you loved the brown.' She saw the far wall, luminous and cool, fresh and alive for the first time. Hughie hadn't been able to wait and finish the preparation, before trying out the new paint.

'There's one problem. It's the ceiling. I used the kettle, you see, to steam off some of the paper. It was very effective.'

'What's wrong with the ceiling?'

'It's on the floor.'

'I've taken the brown curtains to the tip,' he said. 'I've got these from Marks and Spencer.' They had blue poppies on a corn-white background. Fenn could only wonder he knew it was possible to buy curtains from Marks and Spencer, let alone they now opened on Sundays.

Hughie worked on into the evening. As he spread fresh, cool paint on the walls, he insisted he worked alone, without the slightest help, beyond constant mugs of tea. The new study was to be his own creation, fashioned out of a new imagination. As he worked, his imagination grew.

'We could have new covers as well,' he called out, 'What about coral? What's this Ikea place like?'

Fenn was flooded with compassion. The work was Hughie's declaration of total love, his ultimate sacrifice. He'd lain down his soul for her, his intrinsic essence, in destroying the study he so loved. It was an act of love more explicit than anything he could say.

She knew she'd always have to care for Hughie, to protect him, to comfort him, as she watched him destroy what was so precious to him.

She knew, also, as she watched him scrambling up the step ladder to reach above the picture rail, that the need to give to another was a deeper experience than anything other she might have wanted. She was at one with the natural energy of the earth. She was held in a flow of generosity.

It wasn't exciting, certainly, but it was harmonious. She was serene. She had to choose between this and the provocative presence of Lex. Tomorrow, it was unlikely that lunch with him would end with a second cup of coffee.

In his own giving, Hughie, instead of dragging behind her like a child, was now skipping ahead, leading her by the hand again. She wondered where he would go next.

That night, Hughie was strangely athletic, and, for the first time in his life climbed into bed without his pyjamas. Neither had Fenn known Hughie could grunt. She got so hot she kicked the duvet onto the floor, with her left foot.

Hughie left on Monday for his seminar in London. Fenn washed her hair, then spent the morning planning a sample menu for a reformed alcoholic's fortieth birthday lunch. Elderflower cordial featured prominently in it. She also wrote a short note.

At a quarter to one, Lex rang the door bell and got

no answer. He rang it twice more, before deciding that the envelope, suspended from the letter box by its corner, might be for him. It was. He read it as he walked away from the door.

Upstairs, Fenn sat on the floor, below the level of the bedroom window, hugging her knees and trying to control her breathing. She heard his footsteps fade away as he walked slowly to the gate. He paused once, and Fenn wondered whether he was looking back at the house, or digesting the note she'd written him.

She turned and hotched round, so she leaned back against the bed and could see the sky through the window above her. I've let the waters of the spirit flow around me, she thought, and I am content. Jesus called it the love of God. Buddhists call it Nirvana. There are rules attached for these religions. But there must be no name, and no boundaries. A name is a limit set. A rule is a restriction.

I'm not sending Lex away because I want to be good, but because the pulse of the earth lies elsewhere.

I found a pearl, luminous and precious. The pearl is of the material world, and I have rejected it. However, I'm of the material world, too, and shall regret it.

Pearls are thus created; a scrap of pain to an oyster, in time made rounded and smooth, possible to bear. This pain of mine will become a new pearl, within my shell, secret and precious. A jewel that will be with me for as long as I wish. It will never be worn, never seen by the world, a hidden pearl.

# Chapter Twenty-Two

In a snack bar at Heathrow Dodo and Hughie had the full fried breakfast including hash browns. They could have had not only the full breakfast, but prawn sandwiches, shepherds pie with chips, or a tofu salad. Meals were suspended in time; they were according to the body clock. Fenn had orange juice which was very cold and full of bits. Her stomach lurched in pleasurable anticipation. So soon now, they'd be standing against the rails outside the arrivals doorway, waiting for the first glimpse of the girls, home for Christmas. She felt slightly dislocated from reality, as if the juice had been a double whisky. She tried to relax, leaning back in her chair, lifting her head, savouring the moment.

'Everyone says they'll have changed,' said Dodo. 'Grown up. I can't imagine Marie ever being streetwise.'

'Pity they couldn't come before the Carol Service,' mused Hughie. 'There's nothing more English than a chapel full of boys, singing their hearts out. Shall we wander to arrivals, do you think?'

They found a spot by the barrier. Those who met friends and relatives who lived in India tended to arrive at airports in large groups, taking up a lot of space on the rails.

'Twenty minutes to landing,' said Hughie.

His voice was blotted out by an official announcement: 'Flight 106 from Delhi will be approximately half an hour late.'

'I hope it's not bad weather,' said Fenn. She stood slightly away from the barrier, willing the moment of reunion to come.

In Mellowstones, the residents gazed out at the rain, at the sodden garden and the lack of birds. In the hall, Sister Birch unpacked boxes of Christmas decorations, sticking torn streamers together with Sellotape. May was too cold to take her morning coffee in the conservatory, so she had it in the lounge where the television was on, gazed at unseen by those who'd long since lost their spryness.

'We are interrupting this programme with a newsflash,' said Peter Sissons in his usual serious, doctorlike manner. 'Emergency services are on alert at Heathrow. A seven-four-seven, flight A one, treble one, due to arrive from Delhi at eleven-thirty, is in difficulty over London. The pilot reports malfunction of one of the undercarriage indicator lights. The plane is circling Heathrow, and experts on the ground are working to rectify the fault. It is expected the emergency may cause delays in the scheduled times of other arrivals. Now back to our programme on bird-table design.'

May vaguely recalled another such newsflash on the radio. Something to do with a child called Simeon. The rest had perished. They'd prayed for him in church that morning. Strange she could remember that when she forgot so many details these days. She wondered how Simeon was doing.

'Do you think that'll be the plane Damaris and Marie are on?' Pearl asked May. 'Fenn said Wednesday morning, didn't she? 'Spec' there's only one a day. India's a long way off.'

May stared at her, appalled that had not been her own first thought. 'Excuse me,' she said. 'I must go to my room.'

Perhaps she should have gone to the chapel. It wasn't because of the rain, but that she knew God would hear her anywhere, now. She prayed best in the familiarity of her room. 'Dear God, in your infinite mercy, please don't let the plane crash. It's too much pain for Fenn, and for dear Hughie, and Dodo too, of course. Two such young lives can't be wiped out.' Then she remembered the others, perhaps travelling the world in the brave, adventurous spirit of so many young people today. Certainly Indian people too, somehow unlike the faceless Indian servants she'd known, rarely to be trusted, but people in their own right; people May found it difficult to imagine, Hindus, Sikhs and Muslims, all with their alien faiths, but equally dear unto the Lord, no doubt.

She couldn't bear it to happen again, to lose Rose a second time, her child to die twice. She shook her head, as if trying to detach an enmeshed fly. She was in danger of slipping again. Damaris was not Rose. She must keep certain about that.

That other thing, had she imagined that as well? What Lex had said about Lewis? She couldn't be absolutely certain whether he had. Perhaps it had been a wonderful daydream.

May paused before getting to her feet, a faint doubt, like a small cloud in a summer sky, passing over her. It came from thinking about the Indian people. The doubt was not that God had heard her, nor that he may not use his grace to avert tragedy, but that God mightn't be exactly as she believed; that he might, also, take the form of Allah, or Jehovah, even the dancing Siva with many arms.

The cloud passed. God would commend the liberality of her faith, recognize her generosity. There was no heresy. She must have faith, find the comforting driftwood bobbing in the torrents, the certainty on which to cling fast like a limpet. May did cling fast. God would recognize true faith.

'Something awful's happening,' said Fenn. 'I know it is. Little problems don't take this long to sort out. Can't you go and find out something, Hughie?'

'All they say is the plane's circling the airport until it's safe to land.'

'How will they make it safe? What if they don't?' Even Dodo seemed to have lost some of the internal pressure that kept her plumped up and bouncy. She sagged against the barrier like a tyre with a slow leak.

'Pray. That's all we can do,' she said, and took comfort in a prawn and marie-rose sandwich. She swallowed, closed her eyes, and stood clutching half her wholemeal bread. A prawn slid, unnoticed, to the floor.

Hughie said, 'Keep a stiff upper lip. Courage makes things better. Courage.' He stared pleadingly at the arrivals board.

Fenn wanted to pray. She wanted God to be there, to pluck the plane out of a deathly dive and sustain it miraculously in the air, on a safe ethereal cloud, give it spiritual wheels so that it could glide onto the runway, smooth as an angel on skis.

Perhaps, after all, God did exist, and Damaris was to be the sacrifice for her disbelief.

She walked away from the barrier to a bench by the wall, sat down, and closed her eyes. The injured plane circled over her head, holding the fate of her only child.

Eventually her breathing slowed, the arrivals hall fell away from her awareness. Within, she sensed the indescribable size of the Siberian desert, heard the bubble-skin wing of a dragonfly hover. She glimpsed a winter aconite shining in the snow, tasted the blue shadowed mountains of the moon. She touched meadow grass, sweet and damp, and saw a man roam the endless sands, in harmony both with himself and with the burning sky.

Fenn opened her eyes and knew then that the world is turned, not by a man-invented god, but by the spirit of the natural world, as it destroys, as it changes, as it creates. It is turned by the life force, by the energy that is within us all. It cannot be manipulated.

Man invented the aeroplane. He must put his own faults right. The engineers would either succeed. Or they would not.

Around her, Muslims prostrated themselves on their prayer mats, their holy space, for it was noon. Islam does not approve of personal supplication, this would be daily prayer. Dodo had her fingers crossed, Hughie had his 'courage, lads' expression on. A woman in a deerstalker hat flicked her fingers through a rosary, over and over again, in between swigging from a brandy flask.

I can't pray, Fenn thought, I can only hope.

Who knows if her hope, the ethereal energy, the life force, perhaps even her prayer, joined with the energy of those around her, in their longing, in their caring, and held the potential for change? She could never know.

On the plane, Damaris, who had the window seat, said, 'I'm beginning to think it's not trouble with the landing slot, it's trouble with us. The stewards look pretty grim. They'd be giving us free drinks if there was a cock-up at the airport. But they've got to keep us sober, in case of emergency landings. Why do we keep zooming past that tower, I'd like to know?'

Marie closed her eyes. She detached herself from the situation. One day she would reach Nirvana.

'One of those men is looking at us with binoculars.' Damaris felt the muscles of her stomach contract. 'It is all right, isn't it Marie?'

In the cockpit, pilot and co-pilot leaned over the computers, talked into control panels, clutched their earsets. They had circled Heathrow for twenty-five minutes now, burning off excess fuel, struggling to make the third green light show, to prove the wheels were securely locked, and not hanging free.

'Control says the wheels look OK,' said the pilot, Bob. 'I ask you. Look OK? Any fool can see if the wheels are down. But that damned green light's still NOT on. I've got to KNOW the bloody wheels are locked.'

'We can't know,' said Ed. 'We can't ever know. Fuel's almost out.' Ed never showed any emotion. His face reminded Bob of a doughnut, without the sugar coating.

'Doesn't matter. It'll be the same wherever we land, if this damned wheel isn't locked. We'll be bloody roasted.'

'It'll be slower, with less fuel.' Ed might have been talking about a barbecue in the garden.

'Christ,' said Bob, 'this is the last bloody option we've got. Have to face it. You a religious man, Ed? Runway cleared. Fire engines and ambulances ready. Right.' He switched on the cabin speaker. 'This is your captain speaking, ladies and gentlemen. We have a slight problem with one of the wheels, and it might make the landing a little more bumpy than we'd like. We must ask you to take a few safety precautions for your own comfort, and the cabin staff will take you through the emergency checklist.'

Bob switched off the speaker. 'Poor sods,' he said. 'Oh God, I wish I'd been kinder to my mother. Watch my angle of descent, Ed, I've got to keep most of the weight off that side. Right, Control. We're coming down.'

Fear takes people different ways. Two women screamed. A hostess made the sign of the cross against her tailored jacket. One man lost control of his bladder. Damaris was rigid and silent as she leaned forward and clutched the upright seat in front. Before she ducked her head down as instructed, she glanced out of the window and saw the rows of fire engines below them. An eighth ambulance raced to join the others beside the runway, eight white vultures waiting greedily to gather up the dead.

I don't want to die, she thought. I haven't lived enough yet.

The lounge at Mellowstones grew stuffy, and May felt like a walk. The rain had almost stopped, but she stayed with the small screen, alert among those who dozed around her, waiting for the next newsflash. There had already been three, each one saying the plane was still in its limbo above Heathrow.

Peter Sissons finished his shift, and Julia Somerville appeared, calm and doctor-like as well. May waited. 'We have news that the seven-four-seven plane, carrying passengers from Delhi, which has been circling Heathrow airport, has now landed safely and without incident. We will be bringing you on-the-spot reports from passengers as soon as we're able.'

This time May didn't even bother to go to her room. She levered herself up, punched high into the air like a victorious athlete, and shouted, 'Thank you, God, thank you. It's wonderful. You heard. You saved them. Thank you. Thank you. Thank you so very much.' She collapsed back into the chair, exhausted.

'You woke me up,' said Pearl crossly.

In the cockpit, Bob crossed himself, though he wasn't a Roman Catholic. There was still sweat on his forehead and what might have been a tear on his left cheek. He grabbed Ed's arm. 'They WERE locked,' he shouted. 'The bloody wheels were locked all the time. It was the light that deceived us. We got the plane right. There was only misinformation.'

'I'm not a religious man,' said Ed, 'in answer to your earlier question, but I'm always courteous to Plymouth Brethren when they come to the door.' Then his face ruptured and he started to cry.

They waited by the barrier, waited for their loved ones to come back from the dead. Some Muslims were chattering, others silent with delayed shock. The woman in the deerstalker appeared to be asleep.

Dodo whispered, 'Gave us a right fright there, you old bugger. Thanks.' She experienced a strange and powerful belief in religion.

Hughie fetched three stiff brandies to get them through the wait, while baggage was unloaded and customs cleared.

Fenn felt elated, mostly because Damaris was safe, but also, she felt an exhilarating freedom, the freedom of infinite uncertainty. She would never know if prayers had been answered, or if the engineers and pilot had got the plane down by their own intelligence, or whether the energy that created both the stars and the amoeba, and included the spirit of man, had held generous sway. In not knowing, nothing was reduced to the limitations of man, to the smallness of his vision. Miracles were possible again.

Each back-packer, lurching through the doorway, momentarily looked like one's own, then became someone else's child.

At last, at last, they were there, and with no unsuitable boys in tow. Marie carried a huge, inflated Bodhisattva, which she was requested to blow up in customs to prove it wasn't a psychedelic condom filled with illicit substances. The features of the Buddha leered across the barrier, obscuring Damaris. Fenn could only see strands of her child's wild hair on either side of the sacred balloon.

'Mum,' shouted Marie, 'I'm . . . I'm . . .'

'Pregnant?' said Dodo.

'I'm a Buddhist.'

'Damaris, Damaris,' said Fenn, hugging to her the child she'd so nearly lost. The young body clung to her and sobbed into her shoulder. It was ages before they could let each other go. Damaris stood back.

Gone were the black clothes, gone was the white powder, the weird hair colour. Damaris glowed, vital, in jeans and a clean white shirt. Round her neck, on a leather cord, hung an amethyst crystal.

'Mum,' she said, 'you've got a lovely aura. Golden apricot, it's so clear and strong. You're coming over as positive, I can feel it.'

People were staring at the huge balloon, which was about seven foot high, even though the figure was sitting cross-legged. Marie was having difficulty in keeping it anchored.

Dodo said, 'Shall we let that thing down? We'll never get it in the car.'

Marie hesitated, then took the bung out. 'This might be special air now,' she said, 'on account of contact with a Bodhisattva.' The air rushed noisily out and the Tibetan figure collapsed.

Hughie said, 'I wish you'd been at the Carol Service, you know.'

'Dad, that's gone. All that. Gone. Haven't you heard? We're about to enter the age of Aquarius. I'll heal you with my crystal. You're a bit too cerulean-toned for my liking.'

\* \* \*

May stood up. 'That's Damaris,' she shouted, waking up Pearl again, but very few of the others. 'They're going to interview Damaris.'

'What was it like up there? Was it ever so scary?' The interviewer shoved the microphone in front of Damaris. He wore violet cords and a white poloneck.

Damaris clutched her amethyst and said, 'I could feel the forces. They were with us. I was getting good vibrations.'

Marie interrupted, 'If your vibes were so good, why did you keep banging on that it was time the free drinks came round again?'

'Rose,' said May, 'Rose, I never thought I'd see your dear face again.'

# Chapter Twenty-Three

Pru was in the kitchen, her kitchen now, not May's. The magazine was open on the table, displaying the recipe, with its tempting picture. The quantity was for four, but even less than half produced a vast amount of beef chasseur, already murmuring happily in the oven.

Now the kitchen had plants on the sill, and a woven Swedish cloth over the formica table. There was a basket of oranges, lemons and peppers, and a small wooden wine rack behind the door into the hall. Hughie'd given her three bottles of red Bordeaux, and three of Chablis. It was a kitchen in which to create, in which to love.

Pru was used to her new hair, longer now, and she pushed the left side back behind her ear as she cleaned the sink. She wore jeans, which previously she'd thought were too young, and a long marl sweater. She was amazed how different life seemed, that a fear of being alone was no longer uppermost in her mind. She'd cook some rice and make a salad. She'd eat it properly at the table and not watch television until at least nine o'clock. She felt almost happy, almost serene. This morning, she had a preliminary interview with the Head at St Anthony's which had gone well. A youngish master had shown her where to go, opening doors with unnecessary enthusiasm and courtesy. It was pleasant to think back on him.

She was measuring out rice when the doorbell rang, a long blast, confident.

Lex, as she opened the door, was composing an appreciative smile, his expression best for asking favours.

'Would you like to come in?' Pru would once have dithered over whether this was expected, or not.

'My grandfather's coming to stay tomorrow.'

'That's nice.'

'Problem is, Granpy's rather keen on his food. He's going to want more than some muesli and a choc bar.' Lex lifted his head as the smell of beef came through into the sitting-room. 'I wonder if you'd like to come up and do us a casserole or something. You could tell me what to get for it.'

'Something like I'm doing now?' She jerked her head in the direction of the kitchen.

'That smells fantastic.'

Pru looked at his pale skin, crying out for some greens, the look of food-lust in his eyes, and felt the room was warmer for his being there. She said, 'Perhaps you should have a test run. You can stay and have some of the chasseur now, if you like. There's too much for just me.'

Lex closed his eyes, breathed in the life-giving fumes, and said, 'I'll pop out first for a bottle.'

They left the plates in the sink and took some coffee and a bottle of Hughie's Chablis into the sitting-room. The imitation log gas fire flamed enthusiastically. Sitting on the sofa, Pru with her legs tucked up under her, they finished the conversation about Lex's letter. He was careful not to disclose who'd written it.

He'd kept the letter he'd found hanging from Fenn's letter box for two days, then burned it. He wasn't surprised she decided against seeing him. In a way, she was right. He'd been thinking more of her comforting him than anything else. The excitement came from her being apparently unobtainable.

'Tell me why it all went wrong.' Pru felt such a warm sympathy for him, knowing so well herself, the pain of rejection. She felt contented, too, because Lex had seconds and thirds of the chasseur.

'It's bound to go wrong with a married woman, isn't it? In the end, she just let me down. Refused to see me. Wrote a very nice note. I've spent the best part of a year chasing after that woman. Then she says she realized I was only looking for a mother figure.'

'Perhaps you were.'

'Perhaps I was.'

'What was she like?'

'Does it matter?'

'What was her name, then?'

'You're a very nosy woman. A very nosy, pretty woman. A nosy, pretty woman, who's a wonderful cook.'

'Am I?'

'A fantastic cook?'

'No, not cook. Pretty? Am I really pretty?'

'I don't know that you're pretty.' Lex sighed and took her glass, putting it with his own on a side table. 'What I know, is I like being with you. You've got lovely hair.'

'I know,' said Pru. 'I shall always go to Jeremy.'

Lex looked at the woman beside him, whom he'd once thought dull, who now seemed to be spinning alluring spells of safety and of comfort.

'You make me feel real. I don't have to pretend to be interesting.' He looked into her face, and tried to see if he'd truly come home.

'Lex,' whispered Pru, and stretched her hand out, putting her fingers against his cheek, as gently as if she were rescuing a butterfly from inside a window. She didn't feel shy, or self-conscious. She could see

Lex for what he was; quite ordinary under the sardonic façade, no less vulnerable than she was herself, a man who was looking for affection. She wondered why she'd ever disliked this little boy, this child-man, this person to care for.

Fenn phoned Pru at seven o'clock, hoping it was not too early. She wanted to tell her that Damaris was safely home, and how frightened they'd all been at Heathrow. They hadn't got back until late, having stopped off for a celebration meal on the way.

The phone rang for some time. Then, 'Yep?' said a voice that was certainly not Pru.

'Is Pru there?' asked Fenn, wondering if she'd got a wrong number. Except that even the one word sounded familiar.

'She's not awake.' The voice, itself, was full of sleep, carrying a potential yawn in it.

'Is that Lex?'

'Yes, Fenn, it is. Do you have a problem with that?'

## Chapter Twenty-Four

Sister Birch allowed May into the kitchen after break-fast, leading her conspiratorially through the back hall. 'Normally, I wouldn't allow such a thing,' she whispered. 'Guests in the kitchen. Imagine them all in here, competing with their scones. But this is a special occasion.'

'I think of Damaris as my own Rose,' said May, 'and she's always loved the salmon mousse.' Forgetful she may be, but May'd remembered her promise to make another when Damaris came home.

'I'll leave you to it,' whispered Sister Birch. 'Cook won't be back from the market for another hour, and the girls don't come in to prepare vegetables until eleven. It'd be best if you don't break anything.'

May felt insignificant in such a capacious working kitchen. The vast scrubbed table would seat at least twenty people. There was a lingering smell of chicken bones simmered with herbs, and a giant fridge that hummed like a generator stood in one corner.

Damaris was coming for tea, but had to go to the dentist first. Fenn, however, was coming earlier to walk with her in the garden. She said there was something to tell her.

Usually, May could make a very good mousse with tinned fish, but as this was a celebration of God saving

Damaris's life, May knew a tail end of fresh salmon was more appropriate. Corrigan had been obliging, not minding when she rejected one piece as too large, and a second because it was too small.

She poached the tail lightly, just two minutes, with a slice of lemon and a bay leaf. She pounded the flesh with the cream, whipped the egg whites, melted the aspic cube, and saved some of the jelly for decoration.

May wasn't certain the mousse was entirely for Damaris. There was something in her mind which wouldn't be shifted, as if there were to be a Second Coming. She didn't dare to mention this impression, lurking at the back of her mind because it might be yet another slip up.

While looking for the salt, searching in the high, old-fashioned wall cupboards, with their rows of baking dishes and casseroles, she came across the mould. It was shaped like a fish, softly curved to fit nicely on an oval dish, with details of fin and tail. She rinsed it, and lined it with aspic, and cucumber scales. The aspic set quickly. She poured the mousse mixture into the mould. The amount fitted perfectly. It was meant to be, so totally satisfactory.

The mousse stayed in the fridge until the afternoon, but before she went out May unmoulded it and put it on the table in the conservatory. Unmoulded, the mousse was a work of art, laid out on a large dish, with a garnish of cucumber scales under the restraining, orderly aspic. May did a little spry skip of pleasure. The conservatory had become her favourite place for entertaining visitors, away from the jabber of the other inmates. If left in the kitchen, she might easily forget all about the mousse in the excitement of seeing Damaris again.

\*     \*     \*

Fenn and May walked in the garden. It was wet underfoot, and already there was mist coming down on the afternoon with the dusk. 'You're looking very pretty,' said Fenn. May wore a new blouse, blue crepe with a soft floppy collar. It matched her blue jacket. 'Do you know that someone is coming? Other than Damaris, I mean?'

'I'm not certain,' said May, vaguely. 'I may have imagined it all.' She must admit to nothing.

'Dodo was coming to see you, but she's having a day in London with Marie. Marie is taking her to see a Buddhist shrine in Kensington, and Dodo is taking Marie for hot chocolate and Sacher Torte at some Viennese coffee house she's heard about.'

'Dodo is letting herself go,' said May. 'Seems to have settled for food instead of men.'

'Yes, well . . .' said Fenn. 'Now, there's something I want to prepare you for.'

May wasn't listening. 'I'd like to show you the chapel,' she said. 'Won't you come in? I thought you might like to pray, now that . . .'

May went ahead, without waiting for an answer. If Fenn was going to come back to her faith, thought May, now was the time, when her heart was full of gratitude. How wonderful if she, May, were to be the means. She was already the means of helping Pearl. Hazel, the one so heavy-handed with the hair-toner, was short at her bridge table last night and asked Pearl to make up. It was Pearl's own fault she messed up her chance. She managed to curb the unfortunate habit of counting up her points out loud, but wasn't able to resist gleefully showing the opposition her five trumps to the ace. The Vicar too, she'd steadied him up when he was wobbling.

The chapel was originally a stable, but a relative, during the summer, grateful to be relieved of the presence of a cantankerous parent, paid for a stained-glass window and a small altar. There was room for five chairs, two and three.

'Once being a stable is significant, don't you think?'

'I see what you mean.'

May knelt, leaning on the back of a front row chair. She looked up questioningly at Fenn.

Fenn paused, then sat beside her. She had no option, May looking so beseeching, so frail, yet determined.

As May prayed, Fenn tried to let go of the sadness she felt, now that Lex was not there for her. She'd spent with him less hours than there are in a day. He'd challenged her, made her feel attractive. She turned him away, and he found Pru instead.

The lingering regret would pass. She'd stop hoping she might speak to him, stop wondering what he'd say next. There'd be no more provocative conversations. She wasn't certain she wanted to push away completely the thought of what might have happened, had she opened the door to him at lunchtime.

She should be pleased. Pru would look after him, Pru would be happy. Everyone would be happy. Hughie, though, would be ambivalent, delighted Lex was not on the loose any more, appalled he might become related. Even worse, Woodhouse had resigned and the head was rumoured to favour Lex for the post, in view of his excellent exam results. Lex was getting seriously cold feet about New Zealand. She, Fenn, had allowed all this to happen, she'd given Pru space to grow, compassion for Hughie had filled her heart, she'd acted in harmony with the spirit of the earth. Later, the sadness would become a small note in the music, heard by no-one but herself. The wound would heal over, its winter would grow into a new spring. But that was not yet.

May waited hopefully for some sign of the recovery of faith in Fenn, the getting down on her knees, the bowing of the head, the coming together of hands, but nothing happened. Above the altar was an icon; May stared hopefully at the serene face of the virgin and the adult-sized head of the infant. She rather liked pictures in church, was proud her faith could stretch to embrace the Eastern Orthodox faith. The frame was beautiful, gold and heavy. May hoped it was insured. The lock on the chapel door wasn't strong.

Fenn saw instead a four-dimensional image, forever in movement, changing and fluid, unlimited by a frame.

Silently, May, then Fenn, stood up and they walked out of the chapel, arm in arm. May said, 'You won't be going to church again, will you? There's no use me praying?'

'There's no need to pray for me, May. We're both searching for the same thing in the end, you know. It's called truth. Only you believe in your map, and I haven't got one.'

'I couldn't get by without my map.'

'I don't think maps are as reliable as they used to be. There aren't the same certainties, so we cling on to what there was in the past. Parish churches and cornfields, herbaceous borders and Yorkshire pudding, steam trains, and the smell of wet dogs. Laura Ashley made a fortune recognizing that need. It isn't easy to accept there is no knowing.'

'You're an agnostic,' said May, amazed she was able to get her mind round the unthinkable.

'That's only a label. I'm more than an unthinking Don't Know, May. I'm positive we can't know about another dimension. We're earthbound. But it's there, and we need to be in harmony with it.'

'You're a born-again agnostic,' said May, realizing, at last, that Fenn hadn't thrown her soul away, after all.

'That's a label too. I've spent all of this year trying to live without a label.'

'But how do you know what to think? About dying, and pain, and being good?'

'There's no gospel. You have to find it for yourself. But if you free the spirit from the limitations of man's perception, then anything is possible. To know we don't know is a huge step forward.'

'I think,' said May, pausing to admire the winter jasmine, 'I may not be quite so certain over things myself, in the future. All my life, you know, I've been rather set.'

In the conservatory, Pearl moved the salmon mousse to the shelf over the hot water pipes because she wanted to spread out the bridge cards according to the diagram in the *Daily Mail*.

Slowly, the aspic began to melt. Soon it had no shape at all. The cucumber swam free and untramelled. Pearl stuck her finger in the soup and licked it. The flavour was divine.

'We'll sit on this bench,' said Fenn. She wanted to stay in the garden, to smell the leaf mould, feel the dampness, to draw comfort from the cool air.

'You say Damaris has changed?' May eased herself down carefully. These days, she was only spry when she'd got going.

'She's quite normal. She had a shock. I'm sure I told you about my cousin's son, who'll always be in hospital. Ray. Damaris went to visit him, when she was in Adelaide. She was devastated. Now she's talking about being a nurse. He was such a great lad. The accident was one of the things which made me stop going to church.'

'But now he's been the means of healing Damaris.'

'Perhaps he has. There's something else I want to tell you, May. Something very exciting.'

The Vicar appeared at the conservatory door. He came cautiously over to them. 'Just a pastoral, you know. Isn't it a bit chilly out here for you ladies?'

'We're going in soon. I'm trying to prepare May for a surprise,' said Fenn.

'I love surprises,' said William clapping his hands. 'A little party? It's not the day for the lottery coming up, is it?'

Fenn whispered, 'Lex's grandfather, it turns out, was an old flame of hers.'

'What a coincidence,' said William, and had a fresh look at May.

'It's wonderful, William. Much more wonderful than a coincidence. It's a miracle. Love turning out right is a miracle.'

'Beware Fenn, of ascribing divine interference to quite ordinary occurrences. Would you like me to tell her?'

It was too late for anyone to prepare May. Two men came through the garden gate. One of them was Lex. Fenn could recognize his cocky walk anywhere. It was the walk of one who'd fulfilled his destiny. Beside him, came a smaller, much older man, but with just the same certain stride.

They came forward through the gloom. Granpy was old and frail, but with a firm, determined smile. His eyes were wide with uncertainty. He held some yellow carnations, their ends wrapped in a freezer bag. One stem was snapped, and the flower head hung down.

May stared at him, shaking her head in her puzzled way.

Lex came up to them, leading the older man by the elbow. 'This is my grandfather, May. I've found your Lewis for you.' Over the older man's shoulder, Lex looked at Fenn, cold, and somehow triumphant, as arrogant as the day she first saw him.

Fenn helped May to her feet. She would be perfectly civil to Lex when the time came. She would speak warmly of Pru. Her voice would be calm and level. It wouldn't take forever to forget what might have been.

Now, all her thoughts must be for May. The miracle that we all want in our lives was happening. There was a harmony, a completeness, a joy. She must concentrate on May.

'Lewis?' said May.

There seemed a long pause, while they looked at each other, a bubble of suspension while the past caught up with the moment.

William nodded his head several times. 'Nice to see them happy,' he murmured, and put his hands together. 'Perhaps they would like to be blessed?'

Fenn stared anxiously at May, hoping the shock had not been all too much.

'You've taken your time,' said May. She meant to be funny, but knew she sounded tart, as she too often did. She smiled hopefully, her nose wrinkling up at the sides. She noticed his lovely white teeth seemed not quite so secure in the landscape of his dear face, as she remembered.

Lewis stopped looking anxious. He moved forward, away from Lex's guiding hand. 'You've not changed, May. Neither have I.'

He held out the carnations towards her. There were three.

THE END

# PLEASANT VICES

## Judy Astley

'THIS DELICIOUSLY FUNNY NOVEL HAD ME
LAUGHING OUT LOUD'
*Woman and Home*

The residents of the Close were much concerned with crime –
preventing it, that is. With all those out-of-work teenagers on the
nearby council estate hanging around, stealing, joy-riding and
goodness knows what else, it was just as well that Paul Mathieson
was setting up a Neighbourhood Watch scheme.

Not that the inhabitants of the Close did not have their own little
activities, of course, but these were hardly the same thing. If Jenny
and Alan's daughter was caught travelling on the underground
without a ticket, and their son was doing a little experimenting with
certain substances, and Fiona didn't see the need to declare her
earnings from hiring out her house to a film crew, and Jenny drove
home only *just* over the legal limit – well, these were quite different
matters, not to be compared with what went on in the Estate. And
then there was Jenny's discovery, when she advertised flute lessons,
that she could work up quite a nice little earner in a rather
unexpected way . . . .

As the leafy London street resounded to the efforts of its citizens to
keep crime at bay, Jenny realised that it was her marriage, rather
than her property, that needed watching.

'LIGHT, FAST AND FUNNY . . . BY THE TIME YOU TURN THE
LAST PAGE, YOU'LL NEVER BE ABLE TO LOOK YOUR NEXT-
DOOR NEIGHBOUR IN THE EYE AGAIN'
*Prima*

0 552 99565 7

**BLACK SWAN**

# GUPPIES FOR TEA

## Marika Cobbold

'THE TOUCH IS LIGHT BUT ACCURATE AND TELLING. HER
AVOIDANCE OF SENTIMENT MAKES THIS READER FEEL
THAT SHE REALLY CARES FOR HER SUBJECT – A REALLY
GOOD ACHIEVEMENT'
*Elizabeth Jane Howard*

Amelia Lindsey was an exceptional young woman. She had a
grandmother whom she loved, a mother whom she bore with
patient fortitude (Dagmar spent much of her time scrubbing the
backs of wardrobes and wiping clothes-hangers with Dettol-
drenched J-cloths), and Gerald.

Gerald had fallen in love with Amelia two years earlier, when he
was in his artistic phase, and had begged her to move in with him.
Now (no longer in his artistic phase) he was showing signs of
irritation.

And then Selma, the talented and much-beloved grandmother who
had given Amelia all the background of family and home that poor
Dagmar could not give, suddenly became old. As life – and Gerald
– began to collapse all round Amelia, she determined that the one
person who would *not* collapse would be Selma. Fighting a one-
woman battle against Cherryfield retirement home, against
Gerald's defection and her mother's obsessions with germs,
Amelia found herself capable of plots, diversions, and friendships
she had never encountered before.

'AN ORIGINAL, PAINFUL, FUNNY, FRESH BOOK'
*Joanna Trollope*

0 552 99537 1

**BLACK SWAN**

# A SELECTED LIST OF FINE WRITING
# AVAILABLE FROM BLACK SWAN

THE PRICES SHOWN BELOW WERE CORRECT AT THE TIME OF GOING TO PRESS.
HOWEVER TRANSWORLD PUBLISHERS RESERVE THE RIGHT TO SHOW NEW
RETAIL PRICES ON COVERS WHICH MAY DIFFER FROM THOSE PREVIOUSLY
ADVERTISED IN THE TEXT OR ELSEWHERE.

| | | | |
|---|---|---|---|
| 99588 6 | THE HOUSE OF THE SPIRITS | *Isabel Allende* | £6.99 |
| 99564 9 | JUST FOR THE SUMMER | *Judy Astley* | £6.99 |
| 99565 7 | PLEASANT VICES | *Judy Astley* | £5.99 |
| 99618 1 | BEHIND THE SCENES AT THE MUSEUM | *Kate Atkinson* | £6.99 |
| 99648 3 | TOUCH AND GO | *Elizabeth Berridge* | £5.99 |
| 99537 1 | GUPPIES FOR TEA | *Marika Cobbold* | £6.99 |
| 99593 2 | A RIVAL CREATION | *Marika Cobbold* | £5.99 |
| 99587 8 | LIKE WATER FOR CHOCOLATE | *Laura Esquivel* | £5.99 |
| 99602 5 | THE LAST GIRL | *Penelope Evans* | £5.99 |
| 99622 x | THE GOLDEN YEAR | *Elizabeth Falconer* | £5.99 |
| 99488 x | SUGAR CAGE | *Connie May Fowler* | £5.99 |
| 99656 4 | THE TEN O'CLOCK HORSES | *Laurie Graham* | £5.99 |
| 99610 6 | THE SINGING HOUSE | *Janette Griffiths* | £5.99 |
| 99681 5 | A MAP OF THE WORLD | *Jane Hamilton* | £6.99 |
| 99391 3 | MARY REILLY | *Valerie Martin* | £4.99 |
| 99503 7 | WAITING TO EXHALE | *Terry McMillan* | £5.99 |
| 99606 8 | OUTSIDE, LOOKING IN | *Kathleen Rowntree* | £5.99 |
| 99672 6 | A WING AND A PRAYER | *Mary Selby* | £6.99 |
| 99607 6 | THE DARKENING LEAF | *Caroline Stickland* | £5.99 |
| 99650 5 | A FRIEND OF THE FAMILY | *Titia Sutherland* | £5.99 |
| 99130 9 | NOAH'S ARK | *Barbara Trapido* | £6.99 |
| 99549 5 | A SPANISH LOVER | *Joanna Trollope* | £6.99 |
| 99636 x | KNOWLEDGE OF ANGELS | *Jill Paton Walsh* | £5.99 |
| 99592 4 | AN IMAGINATIVE EXPERIENCE | *Mary Wesley* | £5.99 |
| 99639 4 | THE TENNIS PARTY | *Madeleine Wickham* | £5.99 |
| 99591 6 | A MISLAID MAGIC | *Joyce Windsor* | £4.99 |

All Transworld titles are available by post from:

**Book Service By Post, PO Box 29, Douglas, Isle of Man IM99 1BQ**

Credit cards accepted. Please telephone 01624 675137, fax 01624 670923 or
Internet http://www. bookpost.co.uk for details.

Please allow £0.75 per book for post and packing UK.
Overseas customers allow £1 per book for post and packing.